AF541298

The Girl I Know

Sumit Saxena

Invincible Publishers

First published in India in 2018

©2018 Sumit Saxena, All Rights Reserved

ISBN: 978-93-87328-49-5

No part of this publication may be reproduced or stored in a retrieval system, or transmitted in any form or by any means, electronic, mechanical, photocopying, recording or otherwise, without the prior permission of the publishers.

Invincible Publishers

G-120, Sushant Lok III, Sector 57, Gurgaon-122 002

Registered Address: Opposite Kasturba Ashram, Radaur, Haryana - 135133

Printed at Thomson Press (India) LTD

ACKNOWLEDGEMENTS

Thank you.

It's never easy to write while one is working and meeting clients the entire day. First of all, thank you Kanha for making me meet THE girl who changed my perspective and made me realize I can do anything and reach any heights. My family, my mom and father, for letting me write the book and not forcing me to visit home on every holiday I got during my job. My sister, Shivangi, for always praising the story and making me believe that it will be a super-hit one day. My roommates, Saurav and Vaibhav, for discussing my story every day and helping me narrate the story well. Most importantly, my wife Sonali for reading the book during our courtship days and declaring it a bestseller; you have always been a significant support for me. My son, Hridhaan, for loving me immensely. Vikas, without you I would never have restarted my book publishing process. You have shown immense trust in the story. Stuti, for the several times we sat together which helped me overcome day to day challenges in finalizing the book and made me buck up to get this published. Mansi, for helping me market the book on social media and making The Girl I Know popular among the youth. Akshat, couldn't thank you more for editing the book thoroughly. Without you, it would not have been possible. And last but not the least, EVERY girl out there struggling to create her identity in this heavily Male Chauvinist Society.

Boston, Massachusetts, USA

Looking at my watch now and then, I waited painfully for the conference to end so I could finally get something to pacify the mice jumping in my stomach.

Finally, after two freaking hours, the last speaker ended his interminable speech and I headed straight to the dining area where everything looked delicious. Of course, by that time I was so starved that even a fillet of old leather would have looked appetizing!

It was the very first day of my trip to Boston where I was attending a fifteen-day conference. After (over)eating, I left the meeting and noticed it was already 9 P.M. I used my phone to Google the right places to explore in Boston, but sadly, it only showed me museums and historic buildings which were of little interest to me. What was more, most of those tourist places shut down at around six o'clock, so I decided to freshen up and get a drink at the nearest bar.

A short taxi ride took me to Silvertone Bar & Grill at Bromfield Street. I felt right at home. Bars in Boston turned out to be no different from the ones in India, with all the noise and people, boozing and chatting, or simply sitting alone with a drink. *Nothing Else Matters* by Metallica was playing in the background that gave me a familiar, comfortable feel, hearing the song for the umpteenth time. On the other hand, in my own country, I had never visited a bar alone. I missed my friends at that moment and got all nostalgic. Too bad, I thought, time travel is not an option.

Thankfully however, technology has given us a good substitute for such travel in the form of pixels. I had my laptop with me, so I opened it and clicked on the folder labelled 'Masti in School'. The photographs made me smile, until one picture brought back a flash of memory that filled me with quite another emotion.

That picture was that of my best friend and me climbing a tree to steal mangoes from a nearby farm. I looked at him in the picture, so full of life, so enthusiastic, so energetic that sometimes our teachers and friends called him superman. I closed my eyes and thought, buddy, wherever you are, I miss you. My closed eyes hid a few tears as I remembered those beautiful memories and times I had spent together with him. I was still engrossed in those memories when I was brought back to reality by the waiter's voice.

'Your order, Sir?'

I said, 'Heineken please, with a grilled vegetable on Swiss.'

The sadness on my face lingered, making me feel damn nostalgic. I closed my eyes and asked God, 'Can I go back and enjoy those days once more?' They were such incredible days that in spite of limited money, we had unlimited joy. I knew it was impossible to recapture such emotions.

I had already finished three mugs of beer and was looking forward to the fourth, when I noticed a lady sitting at another table. She seemed to be alone and looked like she was Indian too. To be honest, it was a nice feeling to see someone from my own country on a trip abroad. The first thing I noticed about her were the closed eyes. For the next half hour, as I kept looking at her, she did not open them, not even once. When she finally did, they were full of grief. It seemed a little strange, considering the upbeat atmosphere in the bar.

She had on a black top with blue jeans, and I figured she must be in her twenties. I also noticed her black stilettos and a big shinning ring on her finger—probably a blue sapphire. Her loose black hair complimented her round face perfectly. Her chunky blue earrings seemed to dance whenever she moved her head.

Almost instantly, I felt a strong urge to talk to her. I don't know if it was the Heineken or my loneliness that pushed me. There were lots of doubts in my head. I didn't know her. What if she ignored me? What if she was here with somebody? What if she was waiting for someone?'

I finally gave in and moved towards her.

I was almost there when suddenly, she stood up to leave. I turned away immediately, pretending that I was headed somewhere else. It was embarrassing and I smiled, but my eyes followed her till she disappeared behind a massive red gate. I got myself another drink and spent almost the entire night thinking about the old days and how awesome they had been.

***

The next day, after the conference adjourned, I decided to revisit the Silvertone. I was paying the taxi driver when I noticed someone walking out of the red gate out front. I nearly shouted, 'That's the same girl!'

Before I could cross the street, a black car stopped in front of her and she got in and left, leaving me with an unfulfilled longing to talk to her.

The following day, I found myself getting late for the conference. As I rushed towards the second floor, a notice on the bulletin board near the stairs caught my attention: 'Today's special lunch menu from the land of flavours, India! Enjoy the Indian fare in Mystic Blue'. Directions to the restaurant were typed underneath.

Wow, Indian food, I thought, a sudden wave of anticipation sweeping over me. Somehow, I managed to make it till lunch break and ran eagerly towards the restaurant. As I entered the hallway, I was mesmerized by the smell of familiar spices in the air. Within minutes, I was frantically helping myself to the dishes spread in front of me. I got busy eating when I heard someone yelling behind me. I turned around to see one of my colleagues, Jeff, from the U.S. office shouting at someone. He seemed to be screaming at an Indian waiter who was shaking in fear.

'What the hell is this bit of aluminium foil doing in my chicken biryani?'

'Sir, I don't know how it got there. I am sorry for this,' the waiter replied, trembling.

'What if I had consumed this? What if it had made me sick?'

The waiter looked down while Jeff continued his rant. 'Wait till I complain about this to your boss. Who is the owner of this restaurant?'

How rude, I thought. I was still hungry, so I ignored the brawl and helped myself to some more Kadhai Paneer. I turned as soon as I heard a lady's voice apologizing to Jeff. My eyes widened as I realized, it was her again. She seemed ashamed and apologetic for the incident.

Jeff still kept shouting at her, 'You unhygienic and ignorant Indians, why can't you be more careful while cooking?'

I couldn't control myself anymore. I left my plate and went to them. I looked directly at Jeff and said, 'Hey buddy, I am sorry, but it was my mistake. The foil fell from my hand when I was filling my plate. I went to the waiter to inform him, but you noticed it before he arrived.' He looked at me and with a fake smile, he replied, 'It's okay,' and moved to the other end of the dining area.

I turned to smile at the lovely woman, but she looked at me angrily and said, 'You seem to be an educated person. Why did you do this?'

I was not expecting this kind of a comment from her. She hadn't finished, 'Your kind of guys tarnish the reputation of India.' Before I could respond to that, she left.

Looking all around with a foolish grin on my face, I thought, 'Why do I always interfere with the problems of others? I tried helping her and was reproached for something I didn't even do.' The incident, however, wouldn't let go of me. I spent the rest of the day recalling what had happened and wondering what had gone wrong. In my mind, I kept formulating all the things I should have said to her at that moment.

***

The next day, when my European colleagues at the conference told me that they would like to find an Indian restaurant, I did a quick search on the internet and found one not far from our hotel. The following evening we went to Sampoorn Restaurant. As soon as I walked in, I was astonished to see the ambience of the place. It was a pastoral village setting with a water well in the centre, surrounded by statues of Indian women carrying water in *matkis* and men sowing seeds. The waiters wore the traditional dhoti and kurta with a Rajasthani turban. I forgot that I was in the American city of Boston, feeling instead that I had entered the famous Indian restaurant chain, Chokhi Dhani.

Soon after we were settled at the table, the waiter came for our orders. My friends asked me to do the honours, even though I was vegetarian and they were not. I managed to select items they all could enjoy, and when the food arrived, I was impressed by both its aroma and presentation. When I asked for the chef to give him our compliments, he turned out to be from Kota, in Rajasthan. Small world, I thought.

Before we left the restaurant, I excused myself to go to the loo. While walking back absent-mindedly, I accidentally brushed against someone and quickly apologized. In return, I heard the half-whispered word, 'Jerk!'

When I turned to deliver an intelligent response to such a rude behaviour, that I had so cleverly formulated in my head the night before, I saw, to my surprise, that it was the same woman walking away from me!

'Excuse me!' I called after her. She turned and looked at me.

'Is that how you thank someone?' I asked. I was angry.

'Thank you for what? For dropping foil in the biryani with your bad table manners and giving my restaurant a bad reputation among my American clients?' she remarked.

'Look, lady. I knew that guy. He was at the conference with me. I saved you from his anger by saying that the foil was my fault and that I had notified the waiter. That was a lie to get him to calm down. I'm a vegetarian, so why the hell would I be near the biryani? But you asked no questions, just started yelling at me. That's typical of you rich people. You have no respect for who you consider commoners.' My anger vented, I started moving away, expecting no reply from her.

'Wait,' she said, her voice softer now, 'You're telling me that you didn't drop that foil in the biryani? That you were lying to save me from the customer's anger? Why would you do that? I don't even know you.'

My voice was more controlled as I replied, 'Look, lady. If that guy had complained to the organizers of the conference, it might have been moved to another venue next year. Or they might have put out a notice for people to avoid eating at your restaurant. I wanted to avert that possibility.'

She looked me in the eye and said, 'I'm sorry. I should have asked questions. Thank you. My name, by the way, is Mehak.'

'I'm Sumit.'

'Join me for a cup of tea?' she asked.

'Thanks. I'd like that, but my friends are waiting for me to get back to the conference. I have to leave now.'

'Tomorrow, then?' she asked.

'Sure. About seven o'clock?'

The meeting was set.

***

I cannot deny that the hours passed quite slowly the next day as I anticipated having tea with that beautiful, but somewhat sad, woman. I tried to imagine what we'd talk about. I wasn't accustomed to having a drink with young successful business women like Mehak.

Not long after I was seated at the restaurant, she arrived at my table, all smiles and looking ravishingly beautiful. She ordered the chef's special Indian tea and initiated the conversation.

'So you're here in Boston for a conference. Where do you come from in India?'

'I work at a company in Gurgaon, but I am basically from Kota, a town in Rajasthan,' I said.

Her eyes widened, 'Kota! I can't believe it. I'm from Kota too!'

'No!' I said, almost overjoyed with the knowledge that we had a connection from back home. Instantly, a real conversation got ignited about places in Kota we had both visited in our childhood.

'Have you ever been to that place near Chambal garden—I forget the name—but it's near Chambal Ghat,' Mehak asked.

'You're thinking of Karai Ke Balaji,' I said, 'It's beautiful. We used to go there a lot, especially during the rainy season.'

She laughed. 'You know, this one time I went there with friends, one of the boys decided he'd feed the ducks. Unfortunately, the ducks were not impressed and started attacking him. He ran like crazy. I can still see the fear in his eyes!' She was giggling uncontrollably.

I was smiling too. Not at her story, but at the way she sounded when she narrated the story.

An hour had passed with us reminiscing about Kota, when the restaurant's chief chef, Bhola Ji, called out to her, 'Mehak'. He was the only one who addressed her by her name, everyone else in the restaurant referred to her as Ma'am.

'Come here for a second,' he said.

She jumped up and went to him, far enough that I could not hear their conversation. As I waited for her to return to the table, I sipped the last of the Indian tea.

'I have to leave,' Mehak said, as she returned, 'We just got a catering order for a conference luncheon, so we have to prepare for it.'

'I understand. Oh, and don't serve the foil again,' I said jokingly.

Mehak nudged me on the shoulder and said with mock seriousness, 'We'll take care of that, you don't worry.' We shook hands before she disappeared into the kitchen.

***

Back in my room, I started to work on my notes for the conference that afternoon. After only ten minutes of action, I realized that my mind had wandered back to the restaurant—not the ambience or the aroma, but to Mehak. I wondered how many dining places she managed beside the two I knew of here in Boston. Probably a lot. I'd forgotten to take her number, but I knew where to find her again.

Still, there was that big difference between us—the rich getting richer against guys like me who struggled day by day, never seeming to get anywhere. I realized I was daydreaming and got angry with myself. I'd probably not get anywhere, I thought, by neglecting my work to think about Mehak and listen to Jagjit Singh's songs on my iPod.

For the next two days, I concentrated on the conference, not missing a single training session and making notes on everything the speakers were saying. Boring? Yes. But I assured myself that it was all to help me grow as a professional. I smothered my homesickness, my desire to see more of Boston, and the fabulous Indian food I'd discovered in the city—but most of all, I missed seeing Mehak.

***

The last day of the conference went by with endless speeches, handing out certificates and trophies, and all the usual formalities of closing. I had five free days before my scheduled return to India. Homesickness flew out the window as I planned to explore the city further on my own. At eight o'clock that evening, I made a list of all the places I wanted to visit, and found Mehak at the top of the list again. Without a phone number to call her, I took a cab to the restaurant, hoping to find her there.

I felt a little timid at the door, but since she was the only person I knew in all of Boston, I moved in. Without giving it a second thought, I went to the main dining lobby and asked a waiter about her. The waiter gave me a look as if I had just fired him from his job. I asked him twice before he replied, 'Ma'am is not here. What do you want?'

He was questioning me as if I was looking for his daughter at 1 AM. in the morning.

'I am a friend of hers,' I replied, starting to get annoyed.

'You can wait here if you want,' he suggested and left.

I decided to wait for her, so I ordered 'Pav Bhaji'. As expected, it was out of the world. Half an hour passed, but she was nowhere to be spotted. I decided to leave and was about to move when I saw her entering; she noticed me and, as usual, smiled, 'Hey Mr. Gurgaon, what's up?'

I could have lied that I had come for lunch, but I don't know why I said the truth, 'I came to see you.'

'Really? Great. For how long have you been waiting here?'

'Half an hour.'

'Ohhhh! I am so sorry.'

'No issues. In fact, I should thank you. Had you come here earlier, I wouldn't have been able to eat the delicious Pav Bhaji,' I winked.

'As if I would have stopped you from eating,' she smiled impishly.

'Who knows, maybe you would have.'

While going back home, I thought again of the time I had spent with Mehak. She was the kind of person who anyone could easily relate to. Her attitude never suggested that she was too proud of being rich. I recalled that Bhola Ji had been staring at both of us, which I found a little weird, but I failed to guess any reason behind it and simply continued walking.

***

I spent the next two days visiting several places near Boston. It was the third day and I was getting ready to visit the nearby Science museum, when suddenly my phone rang. I quickly picked it up and said, 'Hello?'

Somebody wished me a happy birthday. I quickly looked at my watch and realized that it indeed was my birthday. I had completely forgotten about it due to my busy schedule. I responded, 'Thanks, but who is this?' 'It's Mehak,' she replied.

'Hey, thank you, but how did you come to know about it?' I asked.

'From the feedback form you filled.'

'Thanks for wishing me, it means a lot,' I said in a softer tone.

'Enjoy your birthday and have fun, bye,' she replied and hung up.

It felt nice to get wished, I was in the U.S. and no one back home had my number. Till the point I hadn't realized that it was my birthday, I had been in a good mood, but suddenly, I started feeling wistful. I wanted to call my parents, but due to the time difference, I decided not to. The whole day passed by with no fun. I recalled how I used to celebrate my birthdays in India, how I used to get beaten up in the name of birthday bumps. I was feeling lonely so I decided to visit Mehak, my only friend there.

In the evening, I took a cab and reached her restaurant. I was just crossing the lane when I saw Mehak standing in a dim lit area next to the restaurant. I smiled and started walking quickly towards her. I was only a few meters off when I noticed something. I looked at her carefully with narrowed eyes. 'Why the hell is she crying?' I shouted in my head. She was tightly holding a piece of paper in her hands and sobbing. I decided to go talk to her to check if she needed any help, but when I saw Bhola Ji exiting the restaurant, I stopped. He put his hand on Mehak's head. I had thought Bhola Ji to be just a cook, but now it looked like he was nearly a fatherly figure to Mehak.

Though I had wanted to spend my birthday with Mehak, I decided to spend it alone after I saw her crying, and left. The rest of the night, I couldn't help but wonder what could there have been in the letter that left her sobbing like a small child.

I became very curious, but unfortunately, I had to wait for the next day. I had to leave for India in the next few days, and I really wanted to meet her before going away.

***

The next morning, the first thing I did was dial Mehak's number, even though I was a little reluctant and unsure about how she would respond. She answered just before the call was about to disconnect, 'Hello?'

'Hi Mehak, Sumit here. How are you?'

'Good, how about you and how did you celebrate?'

'Nothing much, I spent it alone, as expected.'

'I can understand. Your family and friends are in India, so you might be feeling alone.'

'I called you to say that I am leaving for India day after tomorrow, and it was so nice meeting you. I wish you all the best, keep in touch,' I said in a low voice, hoping that she would ask to meet me.

'It was nice meeting you too and do keep in touch. Come to my restaurant for dinner if you have the time.'

I thought to myself, 'I have all the time in the world, I am free, and without any idea of how to spend these two days.' I was lost in my thoughts when I heard, 'Sumit, you there?'

Hesitatingly, I replied, 'Yes. I hear there's a place near your restaurant which is very famous for its coffee. Let's go there if you have the time.'

She paused for a few seconds before saying, 'I am sorry, Sumit, but I have a few important meetings today and tomorrow. That's why I asked you to come to my restaurant for dinner. I can hardly spare an hour during dinner time.'

I was saddened, but managing to keep my happy voice alive, I replied, 'No issues. Work comes first. I will call you if I plan on coming, bye.'

I disconnected the call and started to think about the other popular places I could see in Boston before leaving. I was alone and I couldn't help it, so I decided to be happy and enjoy whatever time I had left in the city. I took out my phone to search for other places to visit, when suddenly, my phone rang. It was Mehak. A sudden smile came to my face and pressing the green button seemed to be the most exciting thing in the world. I picked up the call as quickly as possible and said, 'Hi, Mehak.'

'Hi Sumit, are you free right now?'

'Yes,' I replied, concealing my excitement.

'Good, come down to my restaurant. We will go to that place which you mentioned earlier.'

Half an hour later, I was with her. I was happy that I didn't have to roam around the city alone and had also got a chance to spend time with Mehak.

'What is the name of that place you mentioned?' she asked, caressing her hair slowly.

'We are going to Beacon Hills. It's a nice place, I am sure you will like it.'

We reached the place in few minutes. It was a fascinatingly beautiful place with narrow streets. The excellent shops and the houses built in brick in Victorian and Georgian styles were the most attractive part of the area. The cosy enclave was more like a village than just an anonymous city. Mehak told me that this place had its own rich community life and was more popular for its beautiful doors, brass door knockers, decorative iron work, brick sidewalks, flowering pear trees, window boxes, and hidden gardens.

Further, she told me that one needed to get an approval from the architectural commission to make a change in any visible part of the structure. The whole place overflowed with interesting nooks and crannies to explore. The atmosphere was very refreshing. We could see a lot of couples and families who had come there to shop and eat. We had a great view of the city and its various bridges from here. I could bet that it was the most lovely place to end your walk on a summer evening.

After a long walk, we started to felt hungry, so we went to a nearby cafe called 'The Station' and ordered two coffees and sandwiches with extra cheese. Rather than just a simple cafe, it seemed to be more of a romantic place. We were having our breakfast when we noticed a couple sitting opposite to our table. They seemed to be in their mid-twenties. The girl was feeding the guy and was carefully wiping his mouth after every bite. The guy looked unwell and his hands were resting on the arms of his wheelchair. He could only open his mouth a little. Every few minutes, she would kiss his hands and was making him feel very special.

Mehak conveyed her desire to know more about that couple, especially the guy. It was the first time that I was seeing her so distressed. I didn't understand why she had such a strong urge to know more. She stood up and went to them.

Mehak asked the lady, 'Excuse me, I am sorry to disturb you, but do you mind me asking what has happened to him? I apologize to ask this so bluntly, but you were feeding him with so much love that I couldn't resist coming here.'

She spoke these lines as fast as she could. The lady smiled humbly and replied, 'Not an issue, my friend. He is Mark, my fiancé. He was in the army and he damaged his backbone during the war, which led him to suffer from paralysis.'

Mehak had nothing more to ask after this, so she thanked the lady and came back to her seat. I had overheard their conversation, but just to confirm, I asked her what happened. I could clearly make out that she was very sad, so much so she could barely control her tears.

She said, 'I feel so bad for that guy, even though I don't have anything to do with the couple, but just look at him. He looks so helpless, so thin, and so sad. He sacrificed everything for his country and now he has nothing left of him.'

I interrupted her and said, 'No, you are wrong. He has the most loving girl with him, he is lucky to have a lover like her.' I looked at Mehak and saw the tears that she quietly wiped before anyone could notice her.

Mehak replied, 'I want to thank that girl from the bottom of my heart for taking care of this guy.'

I thought to myself, 'Does such love still exist today, or is that couple just an exception.'

For the next 10 minutes, we were quietly sipping our coffee. I casually said, 'You will be amazed, but your name is very familiar to me.'

'Why is that?' she asked.

'Mehak is the name of the love of my best friend's life,' I replied.

'Hmm, it's quite a common name, I guess,' she smiled and said.

'Maybe it is, but you know, sometimes I thank her for being so close to him and helping him get rid of his loneliness,' I replied thoughtfully.

'Where are your friends right now? Are they both married?' she asked hesitatingly.

I was not sure of how to reply to that. His journey had been full of griefs and sorrows, and it took me many months to come out of that shock. I was still lost in my thoughts when I heard,

'Hello, Mr. Lost?' I came back to my senses and replied, 'Oh sorry, I got lost thinking about something.'

'So, I was asking—did they eventually get married?'

'No, destiny had planned something entirely different for them.'

Her face suddenly became sullen. I felt the sudden restlessness in her but I couldn't understand the reason for it, so I asked, 'Hey, what happened to you?'

She cleared her throat and said, 'Nothing. You tell me, do you have a girlfriend?'

'No. I am single yet, waiting for a girl like Mehak,' I responded.

She looked at me in shock. I understood her confusion and clarified, 'I am not talking about you! I meant Karthik's Mehak.'

Suddenly, her mouth opened as if she was about to shout. She was trying to say something, but it seemed as if her words had gotten lost somewhere on the way. Her face suddenly became tense, as if she had just heard the saddest news of her life.

I was taken aback by her reaction and asked with concern, 'Mehak, what happened to you? Please say something.'

I could see her struggling hard to speak. I became shit scared and almost shouted, 'Mehak, are you okay?'

A few tears rolled down her cheeks, then she started sobbing. I simply sat there confused, with no idea of what to say or what to do. I pleaded, 'Please tell me, what happened to you?' A few more tears escaped over the brim of her sore eyes.

She finally uttered, 'I am Karthik's Mehak.'

***

My jaw fell open in shock as if I had seen a ghost. Baffled, I swiftly took out my phone to scroll down to some pictures of Karthik. I stretched my hand to show her the picture. She looked at it and closed her eyes, which was enough to tell me that she was indeed my best friend's lover.

I was stunned and didn't know what to say. Karthik used to tell me so many things about Mehak, how much she loved him, how she was. It was always difficult for me to believe that such a girl could even exist in reality. I had always wanted to meet her, but circumstances sent me abroad for higher studies, and during those very days, something happened which changed everything. Our friendship got scattered, so did our paths. Some have said it correctly, 'It's a small world.' Here I was, sitting in front of someone whom I had always thought to be an ideal woman for myself all this time.

I held Mehak's hand and said, 'You remember talking to me once, when you and Karthik were in Delhi for a wedding and I was leaving for the U.S.'

She slowly nodded and said, 'Yes.'

I waited for her to regain composure and said, 'Can I ask you something?'

She took a sip of water and replied, 'Yes.'

'What are you doing in the U.S.? I thought you and Karthik worked at the same office.'

'Circumstances brought me here,' she replied tersely.

From what Karthik had told me of her, she was a very simple girl, doing an average job. I was amazed to see her achievements and was eager to know what had brought her here and to this business.

I felt a sudden bond developing with Mehak, as if we were both interconnected in some way. The same happened with her as well. She asked me about our school days and how we used to have fun together. I told her our stories and how good our friendship had been. I showed her the few pictures I had with me on my laptop, and she carefully looked at Karthik in every picture, sometimes even touching his face on the screen. When the environment seemed to have grown a little lighter, I said, 'I am eager to know what those circumstances were which brought you here.'

She smiled a little and replied, 'It's a long story, dear. My life is full of ups and downs. You will get bored soon.'

'How can I get bored? I am still amazed and, to be frank, I can't even make a wild guess about what brought you here!'

'It's not as exciting as you think, but if you still want to hear it, I will oblige,' she replied.

'It is most exciting for me because it is related to my dear friend and you!'

'You know, in all these years, this is the first time I have met someone related to Karthik. I can't even explain how good I feel because I've always craved to discuss him, his thoughts, his love for me,' she said happily.

'I can understand,' I replied.

Witnessing The Past

I still remember that noon when I was sitting in the general ward of Bharat Vikas Parishad Hospital in Kota, holding my father's hands and looking at him. He was sleeping and I could feel the pain he was going through by the sudden change in expressions that were marring his face in his sleep. I felt very bad to be seeing my father in this condition, with so many needles poking his veins.

We were just a small family of smaller means. My dad was a teacher in a private school, but whatever he earned was insufficient to run a family of five, so my mother decided to extend a helping hand to him. She was a good cook, so she started a small mess which provided tiffins to students who were preparing for IIT. This was a valuable contribution to the family's economy.

I was the oldest child in the house and had two siblings, Khushboo and Sahil. I was 16 and was studying in class 10th, my sister was 12 and was in class 7th, while my brother was eight, studying in 3rd. My father hailed from Kolkata and was the only son in his family, so we didn't have any relatives from his side.

He had gotten admitted a day before due to severe abdominal pains, and while I was with him at the hospital, my mother was at home taking care of my siblings. While holding my father's hand, I prayed to God for his recovery.

Looking at his face, I could recall our happy days together. I still remember how we used to wait for him like crazy and never let him move into the house till he took us for a ride on his scooter. Sahil used to take the front seat, while Khushboo and I sat at the back. While riding around, we'd scream and sing our favourite rhyme *hurryyyyy chali hamari savari yeeeeeeeeeeee*. Papa used to enjoy our shouting and cheering, and used to join us like a child too sometimes. How can I forget, he always brought chocolates for all three of us.

I was smiling and remembering all our sweet memories when suddenly, I came back to reality on hearing my father's voice. 'Beta, you've been here since last night, go home and get some rest.'

'No, I want to be with you, I don't want to go home,' I bluntly replied.

Papa smiled and said, 'You never listen to anything; you can stay here for 15 more minutes.'

I kissed him on his cheeks to thank him for letting me stay there for some more time. I gave him a glass of juice and requested him to finish it quickly. Like a baby, he obeyed me and finished it. Meanwhile, the doctor came and asked him how he was feeling; dad told him he was feeling better, but still had a slight pain in the abdomen.

The doctor called the nurse and wrote some tests down in the prescription and left. The nurse asked us to deposit Rs.10,000 as the hospital and test fees. My dad asked me to go home with one of our neighbours who had come to visit him, and send mom with the money. I was very aware of the condition of my family, so I knew how difficult it would be to manage the hospital expenses. Thinking of all this and praying to god for my father's speedy recovery, I reached home.

Khushboo was sleeping, while Sahil was busy playing with his toys. I went to the other room where I saw mom crying over the phone. From what I heard, I could make out that she was talking to my *naani*. I took the receiver from her and told my naani to not worry about Papa, telling her that we would soon bring him back home. I wanted her to come over and give some mental and emotional support to maa, which she was actually in need of. My naani really wished to come see my father too, but I told her that we were all there to take care of him so she should not panic and rush here. My naana and naani lived alone in Krishnanagar, which was also one of the reasons why I didn't want them to get bothered with this. I gave the doctor's prescription to mom and told her what the doctor had said. With a fake smile to cover her upset emotions, she started getting ready for the hospital. Being her eldest daughter, I could easily sense the tension she was undergoing regarding the managing of finances between the household and the hospital.

I wanted to help her, but I couldn't, as I was too young. My board exams were about to start in a month, so she asked me to study and take care of Sahil and Khushboo in her absence. I opened my physics book and tried a few equations, but I couldn't concentrate at all. Paa's face kept flashing across my mind again and again. A tear rolled down my cheek and I started remembering the good times our family had had. A few moments later, I wiped my tears and determined myself to study hard because this was the only way I could see in which I could help my family.

I was busy studying when suddenly the phone rang. I picked up the receiver and heard my mother sobbing on the other side. I couldn't understand so I insisted, 'Maa, why are you crying? Tell me, please. Please maa, say something.'

Suddenly, she completely bursted out and said, 'Everything is finished, beta, everything. Your dad has blood cancer.'

The receiver slipped down from my hand and I could feel my feet shaking. Something had pierced through my heart. I was in a state of shock and couldn't see a way out. I was not ready to believe what maa had just said to me. Like an abnormal child, I started babbling to myself. 'No, this can't be true, the doctors must have made a mistake. They might have interchanged the reports with some other patient. Nothing can happen to my father, I will not let anything happen to him.' I couldn't resist waiting for maa to return. I requested our neighbours to take care of Khushboo and Sahil for some time and rushed towards the hospital.

I reached there in no time and went to my father's bed straight away, but I couldn't find him there. Like a small child who is lost in a densely crowded area, I started running here and there, looking for him. In the main lobby, I saw my mother standing in front of a small temple in the hospital, she was crying profusely. I went there and hugged her as tightly as I could. I told her not to worry, as the doctors might have been mistaken. 'Papa only had abdominal pain after all. How can he have blood cancer?' I was trying to convince her and myself with my words.

While sobbing, mom told me that my father was undergoing some significant tests which would shed more clarity on the situation. I left my mother and tried to spot my father. I was getting restless with every minute. Every moment for me was like an hour. Finally, two nurses brought him out on a stretcher. I asked the nurses, 'Where can I find the doctor?'

One of the nurses pointed her finger towards the last room on the left. I dashed towards the place as fast as I could. I knocked on the door; a lady doctor was sitting inside the room. I humbly asked her, 'May I come in, please?' She nodded her head. My throat was fully choked as I was on the verge of crying. In a very shaky tone, I said, 'Ma'am, I am the daughter of Mr. Suraj, who is on bed no. 14. Your reports said that my father is suffering from blood cancer, is that true?' I couldn't control my grief and pain. She came to me and put her hands on my shoulders and replied, 'Don't worry, dear, your father will be fine very soon.'

I was still sobbing and asked her whether it was curable or not.

'Of course, science has done tremendous development. These days, blood cancer is curable if it is detected at an initial stage and your father is on the very 1st stage, so don't worry. We will soon start the treatment and will have therapies later, with which he will definitely be okay,' she replied confidently.

I felt a little relaxed. Thanking her, I came out of the room, a little more assured. My mom was still there with her eyes wet, praying to God; I hugged her tight with an assuring smile on my face. I said, 'Maa, don't worry, the doctor just told me that paa will be fine soon, because blood cancer can be cured. Please Maa, stop crying now.' Even though I wasn't that convinced, I tried to convince her. She didn't know whether it was curable or not, but the word cancer itself was far more horrifying for her than anything else. I requested her to not worry because it had been detected at a very early stage and could be dealt with, with proper treatment. After a few moments, she understood what I was saying and we went to the doctor to discuss what we should do.

After a lengthy discussion with the doctor, we came to know that there were some specific therapies to be done to reduce the effects of cancer, following which, they will get to know his exact condition and will decide if they required to refer him to some other hospital for further treatment or not.

The doctor gave my mother certain papers to sign that had specific clauses, one of which said that the hospital authorities would not be responsible for any mishap during the treatment and the family is aware of the present condition of the patient.

I wondered, 'If they are not accountable, then who is?' However, we didn't have any other option, so my mother signed the paper. I felt completely helpless because I knew how difficult it would be for them to arrange the money for the treatment. I went to Papa and sat beside him, holding his hand. He wanted to say something, but I could feel the pain he was going through while speaking. He said, 'Mehak, you have to become a very successful woman in the future, you have to support our home, you have to become the strength of your mother.' I felt terrible, I ran outside with my wet eyes because I didn't want paa to notice my pain and helplessness.

I didn't want to stay in the hospital without maa, but my younger siblings were alone at home, so she had to go back. It was around 5 AM when I woke up and I felt something strange. I had papa's hand on mine, and his hand was cold. I tried to wake him up, but he didn't respond. A shock wave went through my body. I froze like a stone. My mind had already stopped working and I stood there with no clue as to what to do when suddenly, I felt as if someone whispered in my ears to run and get the doctor. I came back to my senses and ran towards the doctor's cabin.

No one was there, so I ran towards the reception area. I saw one lady sitting there and shouted to her, 'Please do something, my father is not breathing.'

She called some doctor who was on duty at that time. I shouted again, 'Please do something.'

'The doctor is coming,' she replied.

I ran back towards Papa. By the time I reached, the doctor was already there. One of the nurses asked me to stay away from him. They took him to the ICU and closed the door. I quickly ran to the nearest phone booth and called home. Mom answered.

I hadn't cried till that time, but when I heard mom's voice, I burst into tears and said, 'Maa, come to the hospital. Papa is not well.' I then ran towards the OT, but it was locked. I tried to peek inside but wasn't able to see anything. I was dreadfully desperate to see my father, when a nurse came rushing out, probably to fetch some medicines. In that fraction of time when the gate opened, I saw a doctor with two paddles in each hands, trying to revive Papa.

I felt no energy left in my legs and collapsed on the floor and started chanting God's name with closed eyes. Suddenly, I felt somebody's hand on my shoulder, I looked up and saw the doctor. He said, 'We couldn't save your father.' Something shattered my thoughts, my eyes widened, I froze, but I could hear my heart beats coming out loud from within me. I lost control of my voice, I could not say anything, but that message kept on echoing in my mind—we couldn't save your father. I felt devastated and became unconscious.

***

When I regained my senses, I found myself screaming, 'Paa, I love you. Paa, I love you, please don't go.' My mother was sitting beside me; she seemed shattered and it looked as if she had cried all night. She had calmed down by that time and was not crying anymore, but I hugged her tightly and cried. I called my naani and naana to inform them of the saddest news of my life. We had to do the cremation as soon as possible, and some of our neighbours helped us with it. I saw someone very important to me getting burned that day, and that incident killed the innocent child in me.

Without Paa

Within a month of losing him, things changed drastically. My mother used to cry, but not in front of me; she always tried to be normal in front of us. My younger brother was too small to understand all this, so he asked about paa sometimes. When I told him he had gone far away from us and would never return, he would occasionally remark, 'Tell him to take a plane to come back.' My sister Khushboo understood the situation, she seemed very shocked and cried very often, missing him badly. She stopped laughing and playing with her dolls; I frequently tried to make her laugh to help her forget about the loss.

My mom became numb and mostly kept quiet. Her mess business was badly affected too, and all her savings had already been exhausted. She knew that her mess was the only source of income left, so she decided to start the work again. Sometimes however, it seemed as if someone somewhere was very angry with us, keeping all possible kinds of problems in our life alive.

For the mess, we had one big hall on rent near our house where the students used to come and take their dinner. In the afternoon, my father used to deliver tiffins to the students at their respective homes. We had hardly 20 houses where supplied food, which my father managed efficiently. Sometimes during lunch hours, we got a few too many students, so we had hired a cook to help my mother with the cooking.

Our mess was called *Radhe* and it was barely six months old. My mother was an excellent cook, and the students loved her food as it reminded them of the food prepared by their own mothers. We had started getting more students a month ago, but due to my father's depleting health, we had to stop the mess for a month and a half, which resulted in a loss of all those students.

When we planned to start the mess again, the landlord of that place asked us to deposit two month's rent upfront. My mom didn't have any money left so she requested the landlord to give her one more month and described the whole situation to him, but he said that he too had a family to feed and needed money for their livelihood. Mom requested again and he agreed on receiving half of the total amount and start the work.

Sometimes I thought, 'Money has become so powerful these days that everyone is running behind it. My father died a month ago, but all everyone cares about is money. In the end, it was the money, or rather, the lack of it that made us forget all our sadness.' Thus, we started our daily routine.

Someone has said it right, 'Time moves on and nothing is permanent,' but he didn't explain why poor people have to struggle every day for everything, why they have to forget everything else, like who is dying, or who has died, and have to work harder and harder to feed their children and keep on doing this for rest of their lives till the day they die. I concluded that we all have become robots and the world has become materialistic.

My boards were pretty close and I had to study, because in this condition, I couldn't afford to fail and reappear for the exam. It would have lead to a wastage of money and time, and both were of the utmost importance to me now. I decided to do whatever it took to be successful. I didn't want my younger siblings to face the condition which I was encountering. Also, I wanted to give my mom all possible comforts and luxuries of life, as she had struggled a lot for every paisa that she earned.

***

I started preparing for my exams and mom began arranging things to get the mess in working condition again. Delivery was still a big problem, because we couldn't afford a guy to deliver the tiffins. I told mom that I could do the distribution as I knew how to drive Paa's scooter. Mom refused to my proposal straight away because she thought that it was not safe for me to do such things, since I was a girl. I held mom's hand and said, 'Maa, I am not your daughter, I am your son. Don't worry, Kanha is with me. I will be safe.'

She cried, 'Why does my daughter have to face these situations? God, please save us, don't let people see her like this.'

I wiped her tears and asked, 'Tell me one thing, do you trust me or not?'

'Yes beta, who else would I trust now?' she replied.

'So here is my promise to you. I promise not to do anything wrong and to prove to you that I am your son. In fact, I'll prove to this society that girls can also be helping hands to their families, like boys.'

I was determined to change the mentality of this 'male chauvinist society'. That time, when I made this promise, I had no idea about what a girl had to face when she went out of her house to do something, to achieve something, especially when she is alone.

Maa finally agreed and kissed my forehead, but she added, 'I will not permit you to do this during your exams.' I had to accept that, as I had no choice. I knew an auto-driver who could help her deliver during my exams, but I knew that it would prove to be too hectic for her. I cursed myself for not thinking of a better solution.

***

It was the 5th of March and my boards were two days away. I was studying hard for the exams, even though I hadn't decided yet what I wanted to become in future, or which subjects I would opt for the next year. I was studying equally hard for all the subjects. My centre for the exams was DAV school, which was near my home.

Mom had already started the mess again, but it was not running as good as it had been. She was, however, able to pay the rent of our house and the mess at least. We all knew the earnings were not enough to cover our school fees and household expenditures, but we were all silent and tried to find a solution to this problem.

7th March. It was the first day of my exams and if I am not mistaken, it was a chemistry paper. I got up early at 4 A.M. to study. I opened my chemistry notebook to revise it, when I unexpectedly saw Paa's face and went down the memory lane. I had the habit of getting up early on the day of the exam to revise the course. Paa always used to wake up with me, prepare milk for me and sit with me so I wouldn't feel sleepy.

A few tears rolled down my cheeks. I looked towards the sky and said, 'I love you, papa. Be with me always.'

I studied till 8 A.M., took a bath and sat in front of a small wooden temple in our house, and prayed to my Kanha to bless me. My examination was from 10 o'clock. I wanted to look through my notebook once again before I left the house, but mom stopped me and said, 'Don't take so much pressure, your exam will be fine, don't worry.'

She gave me a spoon-full of curd and put a small tika on my head before I left, I touched her feet and imagined touching Paa's feet as well before leaving for the exam. The exam went well, or I could say okay. For the next month, I was busy studying, and I could tell that my exams went as per my expectations.

In that month, I also saw mom working like hell; she used to cook continuously for five hours, then go deliver the tiffins in an auto, sometimes even by local buses to save money. I felt sad when she had to travel in buses full of passengers, just to save some money.

***

As soon as I got done with my exams, I started helping mom with the deliveries. In the morning, I would go to the mess with my mother and help her with the cooking. When I completed my first day there and realized the kind of hard work that my mom put in every day, I wanted to salute her, but I hugged her instead and said, 'Maa, I love you. We are lucky to have a mother like you.'

A few days after my board exams, mom asked me a dreadful question, 'Which subject are you opting for?'

'I haven't decided yet, maa,' I replied.

'Decide what you want to do in future, and then choose the subject.'

I was confused because I was already aware of our financial situation and I really didn't want to take a course like engineering, which involved spending a lot of money. I was thinking of opting for arts instead, and preparing for the IAS exam.

The next day, when we were having our dinner, I told mom that I wanted to go for arts and then prepare for the IAS exams. She was happy that I had finally decided and exclaimed, 'Whatever you do, put your heart into it.'

During my summer vacations, I helped mother with the handling of her mess. In fact, I even made her rest at home sometimes, while I handled the mess all day. That taught me how to earn money and how to value it when it comes from sheer hard work. But even after so much hard work, the money which we made was not enough for running our household properly. Every month, mom used to earn about 10,000 rupees, which was not sufficient. I could see that my mom was facing great difficulty in managing the finances.

The date was 16th July, two days before my sweet little brother Sahil's birthday. Like other kids, Sahil too was excited for a month before his birthday.

'Mom, I want a remote control car as a gift for my birthday,' said Sahil, resisting the food being put into his mouth by mom's hand. Sahil wanted an automatic remote car for his birthday and had been trying hard to convince mom for the last one month. Mom was saving money to gift him his favourite car. That car costed around Rs.3,000 and this amount was very high for a lower-middle-class family like ours, but mom knew that kids don't understand lower class or upper class, all they cared about was their toys.

At night, I asked mom about Sahil's gift. I could see that she was sad. She said, 'Beta, I have been saving money for the longest time now, but I could only collect about a 1000 rupees till now,' and started crying.

'Maa, we will gift him something else, he is a kid and kids are stubborn,' I consoled her and requested her to stop crying for every little thing, as it could affect her health.

Mom, Khushboo and I planned a surprise party for Sahil; I bought his favourite superhero's (Superman) printed shirt for him and hid it somewhere in the house so that he couldn't see it. We waited for the clock to strike 12, when Sahil was already in deep sleep. We all went towards him and shouted together, 'Happy Birthday to you, Happy Birthday to Sahil!'

He quickly woke up and looked at us as if he had been expecting all this. He smiled and said thank you in his cute voice.

I put my palms over his eyes and took him to the cake. When I removed my hand, he exclaimed, 'Wow! Chocolate cake!' and hugged mom. Mom smiled and kissed him on his forehead. Khushboo gifted him chocolates and a Mickey-mouse pencil, and I gifted him the superman shirt. He saw the shirt and started shouting in excitement, 'Ooooo superman ka shirt, yoooooooooooo.'

We were all eating cake when he said, 'Where is my car?'

He had never demanded anything before, this was the first time he had asked for something, but we felt unfortunate that we couldn't get him what he desired.

Mom told him, 'On your next birthday, you will get a car for sure. This time, your maa doesn't have enough money to buy it.'

He was a small kid at that time, but still, he understood maa's problem and replied, 'It's okay, Maa,' and got busy putting on his new t-shirt.

I could sense the sadness in Sahil's reply. I felt so terrible that he couldn't get what he wanted, and I already knew that mom was soon to face problems with submitting our school fees in the near future.

I had to think of some solution, and the only solution to this problem was to increase the earnings. We couldn't improve the profits through our mess, as it depended entirely on the students we got. I thought, 'Why can't I start working and help mom?'

I wanted to work, but I was anxious whether mom would consent to it or not. I was looking for the right time to talk to her. The weekend arrived. We kept our mess off so we could get some rest, and I thought that Sunday would be the right time to discuss this. I was panicking. After all, I was going to talk about working, that too in class 11th. I knew it would be a bolt from the blue for Maa.

On Sunday, my mother was busy with the household duties; I moved around aimlessly, moving here and there, trying to bring the subject up, trying to find just the right moment. I was not sure what the perfect moment would be. I was thinking more than my mind could handle. During lunch, I finally spilled it out. I said, 'Mom, I want to request something from you.'

'Haan, beta?' she replied.

'I want to help you earn money for the family.'

'I don't get you,' she said, looking confused.

I was still feeling hesitant in asking, but I gathered up the courage and said, 'Maa, I want to do a job.'

She was stunned and heatedly replied, 'What? Have you gone crazy? It's not your age to work, complete your studies first, then you can do whatever you want!'

'Maa please, I want to work. I want to become a helping hand for you. I know it's not the age to work, but I also know that it will be tough for you to manage everything alone,' I requested.

'Whatever it is, you concentrate on your studies, leave everything else to me, I can handle it, and if there is something you need, just ask me, I'll get it for you,' she replied.

'I don't want anything, but I know you need a helping hand. If paa were here, I would not have thought of working. Please maa, it will not affect my studies, I promise, I will do extra hard work to manage my studies simultaneously.'

She refused again and asked me not to discuss this anymore. I knew maa didn't want me to work at this age and that is why she had said no. Like an obedient child, I agreed to maa's decision and quit the idea of working even though I wanted to help her.

Summer vacations had come to an end, Khushboo and Sahil's schools had started. My school was a little expensive, so I joined Sofia. In our budget, it was the best available option in arts for me.

Now mom had to handle everything alone. She used to wake up early at 5 A.M. and do all the household work, prepare lunch for all of us and go to the mess. We came back from school at 2 in the afternoon, and mom used to return home at 11 in the night after winding up all her work at the mess. I could only help her on Sundays or sometimes after school, but due to my education, she always forced me to be at home, to study and to take care of my siblings.

This routine continued for another two months or so. One day, when I returned from school, mom was at home. It felt weird to see her home at that time, and sleeping too. I went near her and looked at her. It was lovely to see her resting. I sat beside her and kept my hand on her head to give her a head massage. It felt like I had put my hand on a burning stove. I got seriously frightened and shouted, 'Maa, Maa.'

She woke up with an anxious face, as if from a bad dream and said, 'Yes, beta?'

'Maa, you have a very high fever,' I started crying.

'Don't worry, beta. I have taken the medicine. I'll be fine soon,' she smiled.

'Maa, let's go to the doctor, please,' I requested.

'It's not such a big thing, beta. I'll be fine by evening. The doctor will unnecessarily charge a 100 rupees.'

'Maa, please, I beg of you, let's go.' I tried to pull her up from the bed. At last, she agreed and stood up.

I called for an auto to take us to the clinic. I recalled how my father had suffered from abdominal pains a few times and how he used to take painkillers instead of consulting a doctor. I didn't want the same thing to happen with my mother. This time, I thought, I would die if the same thing were to repeat itself. I didn't want to take a single chance. I couldn't have taken so much pain and sorrow again.

We reached the doctor's clinic in Talwandi. It was already overflowing with patients. A man was standing there with a diary in his hand, writing the patients' names. Our number was 21. 'India needs so many more doctors,' I thought, looking at the long queue. Finally, after 45 minutes of waiting, we got into the doctor's cabin. Mom told her everything about her health. The doctor measured her blood pressure and heart beats and told us about her elevated blood pressure, which was 150/100. She wrote some medicines and a few tests down and asked us to come again with the reports.

We went to the pathology lab for the tests. A nurse sitting at the reception told us to deposit Rs. 300 for blood and urine tests. She then told us to come back in the evening to collect the report. I requested her to give us the reports as soon as possible, and she told us to wait for at least an hour. I thought it better to wait there, rather than come back in the evening and spend the extra money on conveyance.

We sat in the waiting room. I was looking a little puzzled, so mom asked me, 'What happened to you, beta? why do you look so tensed?'

'Nothing, Maa. It's just that I am a little tensed about your health.'

'Beta, nothing will happen to me, you don't worry.'

'I know, but after Paa, I cannot afford to lose you too.' Tears started to roll down my cheeks.

Mom hugged me tight and replied, 'One day, I will go for a world tour with my best friend, I will see you getting married, I will play with my grandchildren, and I promise I will do all these things and more.'

'I am taking you on your word, Maa,' I replied and kissed her.

I didn't realize how an hour passed while talking. I couldn't remember sitting like this with maa and talking for so long without any disturbances, I felt good talking to her. We collected the reports and went back to the doctor's clinic. Again there was a long line there and we had to wait for half an hour.

The doctor saw the reports and told us that her haemoglobin was low. She also told mom not to do rigorous work as that would lead to an increase in blood pressure, which could raise the probability of a heart attack. She told us that she needed to measure her blood pressure every two days.

'If it remains high, we'll have to start the medicines to control the blood pressure,' she said.

We went back home and I told mom to take her medicines and get a good night's sleep.

***

I knew that she would keep on doing rigorous work because we didn't have an option. Due to lack of money, mom couldn't even hire a helping hand for the mess. From that moment itself, I became determined to start working in the evening after my school hours, so I could earn some extra money. I knew that if I asked for her permission again, she would be really angry which would unnecessarily increase her BP. So I decide not to tell her.

The bigger challenge in front of me was how to get a job. I was 16 years old, it was not like people were lining up to give me a job at that young an age. I started searching for options and considered many kinds of work, such as a receptionist at a hotel or a saleswoman at some apparel shop. I even found some companies, got their contact details from the directory and called them up, but everyone asked for some degree or some specific qualifications.

I was eager to do something. I had already been looking for a week. One day, after coming back from school, I was reading a newspaper when I saw an article on one corner of the front page.

'Want to earn money? Don't know what to do? Join our company and earn extra money, we only need a few of your hours.' The company's name was Tele-King Communications. At the end of the article, their number was mentioned. I thought of giving it a try and called. A lady picked up the phone and said, 'Thank you for calling Tele-King Communications, how may I assist you?'

I stammered and replied, 'Hhhelo, my name is Mehak. I saw your article in the newspaper. I want the job.'

'What are your qualifications Mehak?' she inquired.

'I am in class 11th,' I nervously replied.

'Okay, you can come for an interview at 3 o' clock tomorrow.'

'Okay,' I replied and put the phone down.

I was baffled by the way that lady had responded. She hadn't asked me anything else and had invited me for an interview right away, even after I told her that I was only in class 11th. I decided to go there and see what kind of job they had to offer, and then choose the next step. I checked the address on that article again; it was in 'Gumanpura'.

The next day when I came back from school, I quickly had my lunch and asked Khushboo to take care of Sahil for one hour. I hurriedly went out of the house, as it was 2:20 PM already. I didn't have much money, so I chose to take a bus. The bus was fully packed, with barely any place to stand. I noticed that every man on the bus was staring at me in a weird way. I felt very uncomfortable, but I thought, 'I will have to face these kind of conditions at every step; I have to be stronger.'

FIRST JOB

I reached the Tele-King Communications office at 3:10 PM, thanks to the local bus. I quickly ran into the office. I went to the receptionist who asked me, 'How may I help you?' I told her the conversation I had had with that lady over the phone the previous day. The receptionist smiled and said, 'That was me, by the way.'

'Can I have your CV please?' she asked.

'I don't have my CV!' I replied with embarrassment.

She was a little shocked to see a 11th standard girl applying for a job, without even having her resume on her. I asked that lady about the job details before going in for the interview. She told me, 'It's a telesales job opening. Tele-King Communications is a newly opened call centre in Kota. We are recruiting candidates who can do telesales for us, and you don't have to be too qualified for this job. The only eligibility we require is that you speak English!'

'Okay,' I replied and went in for the interview.

When I entered the hall, I saw around 20 other candidates already sitting there and waiting for their turn to come. I went in and sat quietly on a chair in one corner of the hall. I was very nervous because it was going to be my first experience giving an interview, and also because mom didn't know anything about this. I noticed everyone else sitting there; they all looked decidedly older than me. Some of them looked back at me as well. They might have wondered what this little girl was doing there. At that time, I was short, skinny and looked even younger than most girls my age.

I was waiting for my turn. A guy came in every 5-10 minutes to call in the next candidate. I was observing the candidates who were going in and coming out; some candidates were coming out with happy faces, some with sad faces. I wondered what the interviewer must be asking all of them. I thought, 'Every candidate who has come here for the interview must need this job very much. A few of them will get selected and a few of them will get rejected. What will happen to those who get rejected, will they try for some other job?' I recalled a phrase that my father used to say, "survival of the fittest" and here I was witnessing the live example of the very same!

I heard someone calling my name. I said 'yes' and entered the room. A boy and a girl were sitting there. They seemed to be in their 20's. I greeted them with a good afternoon and sat down. The girl asked me about my resume. I replied the same as I had about an hour ago.

'You came for the interview without your resume?' she asked incredulously.

'Ma'am, this is my first experience of a job interview, and I don't know how to make a resume, but I can promise you that I am a quick learner and I will prove to be beneficial to your company,' I told her with confidence on my face.

'What is your educational background? ' the boy asked.

'I just gave my class 10th boards exams!' I replied.

They both looked so stunned as if they had seen a ghost in me. The girl said with her eyes wide open, 'Why do you want to do a job in class 11th? It's time for you to study, instead of searching for jobs.'

I said, 'My family needs money and I want to become a helping hand to my mother. I can manage my studies simultaneously with the job.'

They asked me some more questions about my family and my school. They also told me about the job in more detail, that my shift timings would be from 4 P.M. to 10 P.M. and that I had to sell the products of a company called Teleshopping Networks. They had products like slimming belts, hair oils for bald people, etc.

The girl asked me if I could manage to work in these timings, to which I said yes. I think the girl had a soft corner for me. It didn't hurt that I had excellent communication skills, which was the most significant eligibility criteria for that job. The guy told me that since I was a fresher and still in school, they could only offer me 8000.

I looked at him gratefully and said yes right away. They congratulated me and asked me to join as soon as possible. I told them that I would report the next week on Monday, and left. I was very happy with getting a job on my first try. Also, I felt good that from now onwards, I could help mom with the finances. On my way back home, I was thinking how mom had to work hard, day and night, yet she only managed to earn a measly 10,000 bucks a month, while I would get 8000 for just 6 hours each day. I could easily understand that there was a lot of money in private jobs these days.

The next big challenge was breaking this news to mom. I came back home thinking what the right time would be to tell her about the job. Mom came back home at around 10 in the night. She had started winding up the mess a little early due to her health. I was very nervous and was fidgeting with things like changing the T.V. channels frequently, washing cleaned utensils all over again, etc. Mom noticed me when she entered and asked, 'What happened to you, beta?'

I politely said, 'Maa, your birthday is coming up next month.'

'Hmmm!' she said while doing some work.

'I want to gift you a new saree!' I said, smiling.

'Not now, beta, I will ask you for gifts when you start earning!' she patted my back and replied.

I held maa's hand in mine and said, 'Maa, I will definitely work in the future and give you all the happiness in the world, but you need help right now. I'll be glad if I could help you now. The future is unpredictable, we can't control it, but we can control the present by our actions. I have never asked anything of you. For the first time I am asking for something, please don't deny it!' A few tears rolled down my cheeks as I spoke.

Mom got baffled and replied, 'What is it, beta? Tell me!'

'I want to be a helping hand to you, Maa. I can't see you working all day just to give us a good life. I don't need a good life for myself. You are the most precious gift I could ever have in my life and I can't see your health deteriorating like this. Please allow me to work, maa!'

Mom looked at me with tears in her eyes. She hugged me and said, 'I love you, beta. May God give every mother a child like you!'

She finally agreed. 'If you want to work so badly, you can work, but beta, you have to be very careful because the world out there is not as simple as it looks.'

I promised mom that I would be cautious and would share everything with her. She also told me that I could do the job only for a few months and would have to leave it during my exams. I also had to request my company to arrange a cab for me because it was not too safe for a girl to come back home alone late at night. I agreed to whatever she asked, as I was more than happy to be able to do something for my family, but I was unaware at that time what my destiny had planned for me.

The day was Monday and it being my very first day at the job, I was very nervous. I had requested my company to provide me the cab service and they had agreed. I was getting goose bumps just thinking of the fact that I would be earning very soon and helping my maa, but I also understood that it would be very hectic for me to come from school, get ready and leave for the job. However, I hardly cared, as helping maa was the priority. I thought, 'Now, I have to manage everything. I promised maa I won't let it affect my studies as well. Hence, I will have to put extra effort in studies!'

I came back home at 2 o'clock. That entire day, I hadn't really been able to concentrate at school, as all I could think about was how it would be at the office and what kind of people I would meet. I quickly ate the lunch which mom had sent from the mess. We had decided on this arrangement that mom would send us the lunch from the mess itself, which would save my time and effort too.

I reached the office at 4 o'clock. The receptionist told me to fill some forms. I learnt that her name was not receptionist, she was Shikha. The forms asked me for my father's name, mother's name, address, etc. I felt intense sorrow in my heart when I wrote Late. Mr. Suraj in the form. I thought, 'For the rest of the world, you have died, but you are still with me, Paa!'

I filled the forms and submitted them to Shikha. She smiled and said, 'Welcome to the company, all the best for your first day.'

'Thanks!' I gave her a big smile and replied.

I then went into the office area and saw around 12 to 13 people already assembled there. The cubicles were small. All of them were wearing big headphones and were busy talking into them. There was a lot of noise in the office. It was more like sitting in some food court where everyone is busy chatting and all you can hear is a mixture of different kinds of noise.

I thought, 'Soon, I will also be a part of all this!'

I asked myself, 'How can I perform better? How can I sell the products? I don't know how to sell, nor am I a very talkative person. Let's see what happens!'

I didn't know where to go, so I followed the rest of the guys who had come in with me. All of them went inside a small room where our interviewers were sitting and waiting to start our orientation. They welcomed us and gave a few speeches to start things off. The name of the girl who was there on the stage, was Nupur Saxena. She was the co-founder of the company. I observed her during her speech. She was so confident, so knowledgeable. 'One day, I will be like her,' I thought. The guy's name was Mohit Sharma, he was also a co-founder and the CEO of the company. They told us how they had started this company and how much hard work they had to do to bring it to this level. They had brought this company from a three-four employee's start-up to a 50 employee strong company.

***

They then told us about the work we would have to do. The training sessions were set for the next day. Nupur was to teach us how to sell. During orientation, we were all asked to give our introductions to become more acquainted with each other. Everyone was giving their introduction, like name, qualifications, work experience, hobbies, etc. I wondered what I would say, as I didn't have the right skills, nor did I have any previous work experience. Finally, I got the turn to introduce myself. I was a little nervous about speaking in front of so many people, but somehow, I gathered some courage and said,

'Hello everybody, I am Mehak Srivastava. I am a student at Sophia school in class 11th. It's my first job, so I don't have any previous work experience as of now. I love to read books and hear Hindi classical songs. Thanks!' I ended. I noticed a few guys were shocked on hearing that I was still in class 11th.

We were given the study material of the products we would have to sell to the customers. That day, we only had to study and get a brief idea of all our products.

I was busy studying when I heard, 'Excuse me!'

I ignored the voice and thought that somebody was probably calling someone else. 'Excuse me,' I heard again. When I heard the voice for the fourth time, I turned my head to the left and noticed a guy sitting next to me and looking at me. Since I didn't know anybody there, I felt a little weird about him calling me like that. I gave him an intimidating look and asked, 'Are you talking to me?'

He smiled and replied, 'Yes, can I borrow your pen for a minute. I forgot to bring mine!'

'I have only one pen which I am using,' I said.

'By the way, my name is Saurav,' he smiled and introduced himself.

I was least concerned about talking to him, but I said, 'Hi! I am Mehak.'

He tried to talk again. 'You like sales?'

I had no idea what he was talking about, so I replied, 'No!' and acted as if I was swamped with the studying.

I think he understood that I didn't want to talk to him, so he stood up and started walking away. He had just moved a few steps away when he turned back and said, 'In case you need any help, feel free to ask me!' and left without hearing my reply.

I hardly cared about him and continued with my work. My first day was spent studying. I left for home at 8:30 P.M. Nupur allowed us to go early as it was our first day. I reached home by 9 P.M. and found mom waiting for me at home.

Now that I was earning, I requested mom to hire one more guy to help her in the mess. After multiple requests from me, she agreed to hire another person for the evening shift, so she could get some rest and have some more time to spend with Khushboo and Sahil.

She then proceeded to ask me about everything, the whole itinerary of my day, and I told her the whole thing. I also told her about that weird guy that I had met. Mom heard everything quietly and then lovingly put my head in her lap and started massaging it. She said, 'Beta, I want to give you an important lesson today which you should remember for the rest of your life!'

'What is it, maa?' I asked while enjoying the lovely head massage.

She replied with a serious voice, 'Girls are often very soft-hearted. They easily start trusting people who are outwardly nice to them. You need to be very careful, especially around boys. Now, I am not saying that all the boys you will meet are bad, but a lot of them might try to take advantage of you in some way or another. It sounds a little awkward, but this is the bitter truth.'

'See, us girls,' she continued, 'We start taking their false promises seriously and then regret it later. Make many friends, Mehak. Don't be reserved, for it is only friends who will stick by you always. Everybody else will leave you at a certain point of time, when they are done with their selfishness!'

'When girls make relations with somebody, they put their heart and soul into it, but when someone breaks their hearts, they aren't able to recover from that trauma. So it's better to keep ourselves away from these things.'

I was gravely hearing every word she said. After she finished, there was a five minute silence. Then I spoke, 'Maa, I'll always remember your advice and will make sure not to do anything which might hurt you. I promise, you trust me and I'll need your trust always. I promise you that I will focus on my ambitions and stay away from these things.'

Mom kissed me and replied, 'I trust you blindly and will always do!'

We took our dinner together. I was feeling tired, so I went to bed early. Mom came to me when I was half asleep, she kissed me on my forehead and asked, 'What do you want for your birthday, sweetheart?'

I had completely forgotten that it was my birthday in two days. At one time, I used to start planning for it a month in advance. Now, I was just so busy.

I politely replied, 'I need nothing but my Maa; you are the best gift for me!'

I really don't know where the child in me had gotten lost and how I ended up being so mature and sensible. I think my mom sensed this and replied, 'Beta, it's good that you have started working, and soon you will help me with the finances as well, but I really don't want you to lose your childhood in all this. I would hate myself if that happened." She took a minute's pause and continued, 'It's good that you are more sensible than the rest of the girls of your age, but always remember to keep alive the child in you because it's good to be a child sometimes. It will help you stay happy forever in your life!'

I replied, 'Okay, Maa. You can give me whatever you want, I don't want anything as such.'

I told her to bring me something to make me happy, but from the core of my heart, I knew that I didn't want Maa to spend unnecessarily on my gift. I was trying to sleep as I had to go to school the next day, but a thought kept me awake for some time. My school friends didn't know that I had a job after school and I couldn't even tell them for the fear of censure. The girls at Sofia were known throughout town for their high class attitude.

The next day, I was sitting in class, lost in thoughts. I was thinking about my office, my job and everything else. I was least interested in studying. I was beginning to realize why parents tell their children to finish their schooling first and then start a job. It was proving to be extremely difficult for me to manage both the things at once. But since I had promised maa that I would make it work, I had to come up with some way. With this in mind, I shifted my concentration back on the teacher who was now discussing liberalization.

The last period was about to finish. I looked at the watch, the time was 1:25 PM. Five minutes left, I thought. When the bell rang, I quickly ran out of the class, reached the parking stand, started my scooter and went home. Everybody in my school used to stare at me when I came riding that old black LML Vespa, but I hardly cared what anybody thought of me. I always believed, 'How others see you is not important. How you see yourself means everything!'

'Hi Mehak, how are you?' Shikha asked as soon as I entered the office. I replied, 'Hi, I am good, how are you?' 'We are all going to a movie today, do you want to come?' she asked.

'Thanks for asking, but maybe some other time!' I replied and went in.

I entered the hall and found Nupur was standing there. I said, 'Hi Ma'am!'

She smiled and said, 'Call me Nupur, I am not as old as I look! Any difficulty with the products description brochures?'

'No Ma'am, I mean, Nupur!' I replied.

'Good, so when do you think you can start interacting with the customers?' she asked.

'In two or three days, I guess!' I replied confidently.

'Good, once you are done with studying, let me know. We'll sit together and prepare a script for the calls. You can sit there…' She pointed towards a cubicle at the end of the room.

'Sure, I'll let you know,' I said and went to my cubicle. I opened the brochures to study when Nupur came back to me and asked, 'Do you know why we selected you even though you have no qualifications?'

'No,' I replied.

'Because I was the same age as you when I started working, but I couldn't get any jobs because I was just in class 11th. That day I decided to start my own company and always give a chance to the ones who deserve it, and you deserve this job.'

I was feeling awkward calling her Nupur instead of Ma'am, so I tried to use her name as less as possible. 'Thanks, I'll work hard and won't let you down!' I replied.

Nupur's words were no less than inspiration for me; I got more passionate to achieve something in my life. I was busy in reading about a professional garment steamer iron and its advantages over other irons present in the market, when somebody said, 'Busy studying, as usual?' I looked up and saw the same guy from the previous day who had asked me for a pen.

I became irritated and replied, 'Yes, what else?' and looked down again.

'All the best!' he said and walked away.

'Why does he always do that? Mom told me about these kind of boys and how they try to be sweet to your face. I should maintain distance,' I thought.

After about half an hour, I began to get bored. I saw a girl sitting in a cubicle diagonally opposite to me. She was talking to a customer and was explaining to him the benefits of using some product. She was requesting him to buy it and give it a try, describing everything in detail. She was sounding so eager to sell the product so that she could get commission out of it. We got a commission for every product we sold; so the more you sell, the more money you make.

Everyone sitting in that hall was trying to sell products by convincing customers; some hung up the calls with smiling faces, while some with sad looks. I could easily make out their frustration and eagerness to sell. 'Money is the most powerful thing on earth,' I thought. A few minutes later, Nupur came to the hall and announced the birthday of a colleague, named Anchit. Everyone gathered at the conference hall to cut the cake. In my office, everybody's birthday was celebrated like this.

Anchit stood in the middle of everybody who had gathered, wearing a birthday cap and with a plastic knife in his hand. Everybody started singing the birthday song for him. He smiled like a small child, desperately waiting to eat his cake. Mohit sir came forward and put some cake on Anchit's face, while everybody clapped and cheered him on. I found myself laughing a lot seeing all this; I didn't know when I had last smiled like that. I was enjoying my new office environment very much.

I came back home and was very tired after all the studying, doing it continuously from 7 in the morning to 10 in the night. I hugged my mom and gave some chocolates to Khushboo and Sahil. Then all four of us had our dinner together. It's good to be with family after a long tiring day. I missed my dad and wondered if dad could be there with us.

I was tired, so I went to sleep straight away. I was in a deep sleep when I felt someone's hands on my head. I opened my eyes and saw mom, Khushboo and Sahil standing there. I didn't have any idea what the matter was and why they had woken me up in my sleep. Mom kissed me on my cheek and said, 'Happy birthday, my angel!'

I had completely forgotten about my birthday, so I was astonished. Khushboo came to me and said, 'Didi, I made something for you,' and gave me a sweet card that she had made herself. I opened the card, which had this written inside: 'Didi, I love you very much, more than Sahil, you are the best sister in the world!' I hugged her for those beautiful lines from her tiny hands. Sahil put his hand in his pocket and took out a pen and said, 'Didi, you can write with this pen in your office.' I saw that pen and my eyes got wet. I kissed him and said, 'You are the best bro in the world.'

Even Mom didn't know about the card and the pen which Khushboo and Sahil got for me; she was also astonished to see the effort that the kids had made for their sister. Mom shouted, 'Now, it's my turn,' and told me to go and check my school bag. I stood up quickly and ran to my bag. I opened it and started to search for my gift in it. I searched all the pockets, but couldn't found anything. I looked towards mom in confusion, but she just smiled and said, 'Keep searching, beta.' I finally thrust my hand into the last pocket and found a small box wrapped in a coloured sparkly gift wrapper. I tore the gift wrapper open and when I finally opened the box, my eyes were left wide open. It was a sweet pink coloured mobile. I couldn't believe my eyes and was delighted. On the other hand, the thought of the expenditure that mom must have had to make for it upset me. I hugged her and said, 'Thanks mom, but why did you buy such an expensive gift?'

'Beta, you have started going to office. If I want to talk to you while you are at office or when you are on your way, how would I have contacted you? Now we can call each other at any time.' She smiled and kissed me.

I didn't say anything because I didn't want to hurt mom. She had bought the phone for me with so much love. I thought, 'All moms are like that. She must have been saving money all this time, travelling by bus to cut expenses, just so she could buy me a phone. No one can repay the love that mothers give to their children.'

***

I had the pleasure of making my first successful sale on the 28th of July. I opened my account with a mixer. Nupur announced my sale and everybody clapped for me. I felt extremely happy and confident that I could do something good with my life. That was the first time when I gained the sales perspective and felt the contentment that a sales guy feels after selling something.

The story of how I made my first sale is pretty interesting. My first customer was an old guy actually. I called a number I got from the database. A guy picked up the phone. Initially, his voice didn't sound very old. I greeted him and started explaining the product to him. I told him, 'Sir, this is a very good product, anyone can use it easily. If you want to help your wife, you can help her with the chopping of vegetables while she cooks. You can also prepare juices in this mixer. I can imagine how much effort your wife must put into preparing food for the family after coming back from office!' I said all this nonstop in a few seconds.

The guy on the other side laughed and replied, 'Dear, I am an 80 year old man and my wife is 75 years old. She can hardly walk, and you are sending her to office!' He laughed loudly.

I opened my mouth in a state of shock. I whispered, 'I am sorry, sir, it's just that your voice sounded like a young lad's, I am sorry.'

He sniggered again and said, 'Don't be sorry, young lady, I like your confidence. I will buy it and present it to my wife, I want to see her reaction!' He guffawed loudly again, and that is how I closed my first sale.

I was doing well as I had sold 18 products in a month, which was a great achievement according to Nupur. Now, I was better acquainted with everyone at office. Everyone baptized me as a little master because I was the youngest among them all. I was effectively balancing my studies with the job. I used to study for an hour after coming back from school and study after returning from office as well.

I learned the sales tactics from Nupur, she had become a good friend of mine. One thing which didn't change was the weird encounters with Saurav. He always tried to talk to me by different means. I hinted to him many times that I was not interested in talking to him, but he never stopped trying. Although, he never tried to flirt with me. He seemed to be a very well brought-up boy, but I never felt like talking to him, so I avoided him most of the times.

***

The day was Friday. It was the last day of the month and I was excited right from the moment I entered the office. I was to get my first salary that day, my first earnings from my own hard work. In fact, everyone around me looked happy that day. I thought, 'The last day of the month is a happy day, not only for myself, but for everybody.'

I was eagerly waiting for my salary. The time was already 8 PM, only a few hours left before I went back home. Finally, Mohit Sir came in and started distributing salary cheques to everybody. I was not sure how much money I would get because apart from my basic salary of Rs. 8000, I had sold around 28 products and I was expecting a commission for those products too. He was distributing cheques line by line. A few minutes later he came to me, smiled and said, 'Congratulations! It is your first salary, you did a good job,' and handed me my salary cheque.

I quickly looked at the amount, it was Rs. 12000. At that moment, I felt extremely happy and could easily feel the satisfaction anyone would feel after having earned something with such hard work.

On the way back home, I told Vishnu bhaiya, my cab driver, to stop at Jodhpur sweets. It was the most famous sweet shop in Kota. I bought a kilo of 'Kaju Katli', mom's favourite sweet. I reached home and quickly ran in to find mom and my siblings waiting for me for dinner. I told mom to close her eyes and put the cheque in her hands. She opened her eyes, saw the cheque and started crying. I wiped her tears and asked her why she was crying. She told me how proud she was of me as I had already earned my first salary at such a tender age. I thought, 'Now our financial condition will be better,' and smiled.

The next day, I bought a few gifts for Sahil and Khushboo. Mom hired another guy to take care of the mess so that we could expand a little more. I felt like a queen, as if I had just won a lottery of a crore rupees. I felt independent and mature.

Sometimes, when you know you are independent, or when you are very happy, you unintentionally do something which you regret later. One day, I was struggling with a customer. I was giving her the description of a recently launched product, but instead of listening to me, she started shouting at me for having called and disturbed her. She was very rude to me, which is why I got agitated and sat quietly after I hung up the phone. Suddenly, Saurav came and said, 'Hi, Mehak!'

I was very upset and not interested in talking to him as usual, so I didn't reply.

He again said, 'Hi!' and asked me why I was sitting like that.

I was so pissed off that I shouted angrily at him, 'Can't you see I am not interested in talking to you? Don't you have anything to do apart from coming and talking to me daily? Get the hell out of here!' I had shouted so loud that everyone heard my voice and started staring at us.

He looked at me with a sad face and left. Finally, when I cooled down, I regretted shouting at him like that. He had always been sweet to me while I ignored him daily, yet he came to me and said hello. I had never talked to anyone like that before. From that day onwards, he never spoke to me again. Even if we came in front of each other coincidently, he would ignore me and walk away.

I felt very bad about that because ignoring him daily had become a kind of habit for me. Sometimes, I even waited for him to come say hi to me so I could shoo him away. I had started feeling special, and perhaps a little arrogant too, because of his attention. I was sorry I had talked to him like that, but never had the guts to apologize to his face. Until one day.

I was at office as usual, busy trying to sell products, but that day was not a good day for me, I think. It was already 7 P.M. and even after making a myriad of calls all afternoon, I was unable to sell a single product. Sometimes, customers hung up the phone saying, 'I am busy, call me later!' Sometimes, they hung up the phone without even saying a word.

I thought, 'Why don't others take salespeople seriously, why do they always treat them like desperate beggars?' That day, for the first time, I felt the pressure of work. I was exhausted, so I went out to get some coffee. I had hardly taken the first sip when my phone rang. It was mom. I picked up the phone and said, 'Hello, Maa?'

'Can you come home right now, Mehak?' Mom was panicking and I could feel her voice shaking.

'Yes, mom. But what happened, please tell me?' I quickly replied.

'Sahil met with an accident. We are taking him to the hospital. Please come directly to Sudha hospital,' she said and hung up the phone.

I ran inside the office and went to Mohit sir to request for a cab to drop me to the hospital. He said, 'Mehak, don't worry. I'll arrange for it right now!' He called the cab driver. He hung up the phone and said, 'The driver is not in the office, but he is coming in half an hour, most probably.'

I shouted and told Mohit sir that I couldn't wait for half an hour. Suddenly, I heard a voice, 'Would you mind if I drop you to the hospital?'

I turned my face and saw that it was Saurav. He used to sit next to Mohit sir's cubicle, so he was listening to everything. Despite my rude behaviour to him, he offered to help me. With a panicky voice, I said, 'Thanks for offering, let's go.'

He lived near our office, so he used to commute on his bike. Five minutes later, I was with him on his bike and we were on our way to the hospital. I was very tense as all I could think about was Sahil. I requested him to speed up his bike. Finally, after 10 minutes, we reached the hospital. I called mom from Sudha Hospital's main gate. Mom told me to come to room number five on the first floor. In that rush, I forgot all about Saurav. I ran as fast as I could. Mom was standing right outside the room. I quickly asked, 'What happened to Sahil?' while trying to breathe.

'He was playing and running on the road when he was hit by a speeding bike. His head is bleeding like anything,' mom replied while crying.

'You talked to the doctors?' I enquired.

'Yes, they said Sahil would require a few stitches.'

'Where is Sahil?'

'He is inside. The doctors gave him a little anaesthesia to reduce the pain.'

Suddenly, the nurse came out of the room and asked mom to bring some medicines and injections. I took the prescription from her and turned to find Saurav standing there. He said, 'I'll get the medicine, you please take care of aunty!'

Without waiting for my reply, he took the prescription from my hand and went downstairs to the medical shop. Mom asked, 'Is he your colleague?'

'You remember that incident I told you from the first day I joined, the pen incident. He was the one.'

'He seems alright,' Mom said in a low voice.

A few minutes later, Saurav came back with the medicines and I handed them to the nurse. We were standing in front of that room when we saw the doctor come out. I asked, 'How is Sahil?'

'We had to give him 8 stitches on his forehead. Nothing to worry about, he'll be fine,' he replied, unruffled.

I went in. Sahil was there, smiling like nothing had happened.

I hugged him tightly. He smiled and said, 'You know, Didi, I didn't even cry when I was getting the stitches.'

'You are my brave boy!' I kissed him on his cheek.

I felt exhilarated when I saw him smiling. 'How brave he is!' I thought.

Mom was also satisfied seeing Sahil beautiful and happy. I came out and saw Saurav still standing there. I gathered up all my courage and said, 'I am sorry, Saurav, for being so discourteous to you that day. I tried so many times to apologise, but somehow, I couldn't.'

He chuckled and replied, 'Forget it, Mehak. It's okay.'

I mumbled, 'Thanks for helping me.'

'The pleasure is absolutely mine, Ma'am!' he sniggered and left.

The doctor told us to come back in 10 days to get the stitches removed. Then we took Sahil home. On our way back, I was feeling so tranquil as if I had just survived some big accident myself. I felt a sense of calmness seeing my little brother safe and sound.

***

I reached office the next day, and the first thing I did was go to Saurav and say, 'Hi!' like he used to every day.

He was surprised and replied, 'Hey, hi, how is Sahil?'

'He is fine and thanks for helping me yesterday,' I said.

He admonished me for saying thank you again. 'No sorry and no thank you in friendship,' he winked at me. He stammered and said, 'Friends?' and stretched his hands towards me for a handshake.

I guffawed, shook hands with him and replied, 'Friends!'

Now that I had atoned for my bad behaviour with Saurav, I came back to my seat and started working. Nupur came to me after a few minutes and said, 'Mehak, your target for this month is 30 products, make sure you achieve it!'

I thought indignantly, '30 products in a month? That means at least 1 product daily! Why are the targets always so unachievable and unjustified!'

I was determined to achieve my target nonetheless, so I bucked up and started working hard. I was making 70 calls on an average day, in order to attain the sales goal. I looked at my watch—the time was 8 o'clock. I badly wanted some coffee. As I stood up, I saw Saurav with a cup of coffee in his hand. He said, 'Coffee for my new friend!'

I was stunned for a moment, how could he have known that I wanted coffee? To be frank though, I felt pretty exhilarated to have it.

I thanked Saurav and said, 'Coffee is exactly what I wanted! How did you know?'

'A friend is connected directly from the heart, it doesn't require verbal instructions to do something!' he said in a flattering way.

His comment made me remember mom's advice and instructions, so I admonished him and said, 'Don't try to flirt with me, Saurav!'

He ignored my comment and asked, 'May we go for dinner sometime?' I could sense the seriousness in his eyes.

I thought it was corny and replied ambiguously, 'Saurav, thanks for the invitation, but I think this is a bad idea. We are friends, and that's it. This dinner idea doesn't make sense to me!'

He whispered, 'Can't two friends go for dinner together? What's wrong in that?'

I owed him a thanks for the help he did, so I said, 'Okay, but the treat is on me.'

He became stupefied and replied, 'Okay. Is tomorrow fine for you?'

I teasingly replied, 'As if you care whether it's fine for me or not!'

'I am not forcing you to dinner. If it's not fine for you, let's drop the plan,' he despondently responded.

'You are such a kid, tomorrow is done,' I guffawed.

He smiled like a little kid who had just got a whole bunch of chocolates. His eyes shined with cheerfulness and he triumphantly exclaimed, 'Thanks!' and left.

On my way back home, I bought some chocolates for Sahil and made sure that I purchased 'Cadbury's Fruit and Nut', 'Bourneville Almonds' and 'Cadbury Silk', which Sahil liked the most. I reached home at 10:30 PM. Sahil was taking rest, but as soon as he heard me coming, he opened his eyes and gave me anticipatory looks. I acted like I was ignoring him and started talking to mom, but I could easily see the eagerness in his eyes. After playing around for some time, I finally gave him the chocolates. Khushboo was sitting on the other side of the room, waiting for her piece of chocolate too. I looked at her, she smiled, and I threw a pack towards her. Mom always scolded me when I brought them chocolates. That day as well, she started shouting at me while making chapattis. 'This can result in tooth cavities, and they don't even brush twice a day, so you better stop bringing them chocolates daily.'

I ignored her suggestions, like every kid does when it comes to chocolates. We had our dinner, I was thinking about telling mom about my dinner with Saurav, but then I felt that she might not like me going out with him, so I decided not to say anything. I was lying on my bed and trying to sleep when I thought about dinner the next day. This would be the first time that I would go out with a boy. 'I am not a little girl now.' The thought popped up in my mind, which brought a smile to my face.

The next day, after I came back from school, I took a whole hour to get ready. I didn't know why I was thinking so much, of what to wear or what not to wear. It was just a small private dinner, not some big party, but all I wanted was to look good. Suddenly, the girl in me wanted to look beautiful, enticing and eye-catching. I wondered if every girl in her adolescence felt like this. Finally, after struggling and noticing that I didn't have many decent clothes to wear, I wore a simple grey suit which I had recently bought. I preferred to keep my hair open that day and even used a lipstick for the first time in my life. I saw myself from top to bottom in the mirror and thought I looked gorgeous and chuckled.

As soon as the clock struck 9, I stood up and came out of the office. I tried to spot Saurav in the office parking lot, but he was not there. All of a sudden, I saw him standing outside the office gate, smiling at me. I reached there and said, 'Let's go.' I was looking for his bike but it was not there. He replied, 'Sure, let's go!'

I looked at him mockingly and said, 'We will go, but where is your bike?'

He sniggered and ushered me towards a car at the rear. I didn't anticipate that, so I become dazed and asked, 'What?'

'How could I take such a beautiful girl out for dinner on a bike?' he stammered.

I felt flattered and smiled.

'So, where are we going?' I asked him.

'You said you are giving me a treat, so you decide. I don't know!' he hastily replied.

I said ambiguously, 'Where are you going when you don't even know where to eat?'

'I like driving, and it'll become all the more interesting with you here!'

I nudged him and said, 'Okay, let's go to Eatos. I can only afford that.'

He said, 'Okay!' and turned his car.

'By the way, whose car is this?' I asked.

'It's my father's!'

'You seem to be pretty rich, then why are you working at a call centre?'

'Yes, my father is rich, but I want to be independent, so I started working to earn money,' he replied.

He told me that he avoided taking money from his father. He had even bought his motorbike from the money that he had earned himself by working. He also told me that his mother and father were very compassionate. They didn't try to convince him against working, since they felt that he was doing the right thing and always appreciated his thoughts. His father owned a few restaurants in Kota and one of his companies was the most significant supplier of cooking oil in Rajasthan.

I started respecting him for his thought process and hardworking nature. We reached Eatos in about 20 minutes. I was ravenous, so I quickly ordered something to eat for both of us. Saurav was looking at me, or rather staring at me, differently. Finally, he said, 'Mehak, I want to tell you something.'

I said, 'What?' while nibbling on the cheese pizza.

He put his hand in his pocket and took out a small shining box and gave it to me. I asked warily, 'What's this?'

He slowly whispered, 'I am in love with you, Mehak!'

I cringed and retorted, 'What, are you crazy?' I looked away. Then I turned back at him, but I was speechless.

'I am sorry if I am hurting you, but believe me, since the first day I saw you at the orientation, I fell in love with you, your cuteness, your confidence, while you spoke that day. I felt something different in my heart when I first saw you. I know, I hardly know you and it's only been a month since I first saw you, but I have never felt like this before. This is the first time in my life that I am saying "I love you" to someone.' He was looking directly into my eyes and I could quickly sense the sincerity in his.'

'Please stop, Saurav, you have said enough!' I shouted.

Everybody else sitting there stared at us as if they had caught us kissing at a public place. I lowered my voice and said, 'How could you say something like that, you hardly know me. Listen Saurav, you are a good friend and that's it. I don't have any feelings for you, so it's better that you forget all this, or else I'll stop talking to you from now on.'

A tear rolled down from his eyes. It was weird for me to see a guy crying, but I was very clear about my mom's advice, and I didn't have any feelings for Saurav anyway. I said no straightaway and admonishing him, telling him not to bring this topic up again in future.

He wiped his tears, said sorry again and promised not to mention it anymore. I asked the waiter for the cheque, but he just looked at me astonished and said, 'Ma'am, you are with Saurav baba, how can we charge you?' and left.

I shrugged and looked at Saurav doubtfully. He was in no mood to discuss anything, so he stood up and went outside. I asked him about what had just happened while we were going back, but he didn't utter a single word. Finally, I reached home. Stepped out of his car, I said, 'Bye!'

He finally replied, 'That was my father's restaurant!' and left.

I was surprised by the series of incidents that had happened. I thought, 'Why did I choose Eatos out of so many restaurants in Kota? What an unusual coincidence!' I lied to mom about having gone out with Saurav, and had to eat dinner all over again which almost burst my stomach. I went to bed early that day because of the jolt that Saurav had given me two hours ago. I had never imagined that he had feelings for me. He had been a good boy and I liked him very much as a friend. I concluded that I had done the right thing and would always try to keep out of such things in future as well.

The next day, when I went to office, I tried looking for Saurav, but he was not there. I wanted to say sorry for having shouted at him the previous day. I then got busy with my work. A few hours later, I saw him crossing my cubicle. I quickly stood up to go and talk to him. He was talking to Mohit sir so I came back to my seat and waited for him to get free. After calling three customers, I went to see if he was free, but he was not there in the office at all. I asked one of my colleagues about him, but he didn't know where he was either. I decided to talk to him the next day. I wanted to call him, but thought that it might not be a good idea, so I dropped the plan.

I waited for him the next day as well, but he didn't turn up. I felt something was fishy, so before leaving for home that day,

I went to Mohit sir and asked about him. Mohit sir paused for a second and then told me that he had resigned.

I was stunned. I felt sorry about that day, but I hadn't done anything wrong to him, I thought. I had only told him what I truly felt for him. I decided not to call him as that would have just made things nastier.

THE UNFORTUNATE DAY

The day was 'Durga Ashtami'. I still remember the date, it was the 23rd of September. My school was off that day, so from the morning onwards, mom and I got busy preparing for the Pooja. We completed the preparations and did the 'Hawan'. On this day every year, we used to make a few packets of food and distribute them among the beggars and other poor people we found on the roads. We prepared 20 packets of food, which contained Daal, Sabzi, Roti, Rice, and a Sweet. Mom and I went out and distributed those packets at this place called 'Gayatri Bhavan'. All the beggars usually waited there for food, as this trust fed them daily, so we decided to contribute something to their excellent endeavour and gave them those 20 packets to distribute.

On our way back home, mom said, 'Why don't you take a leave from office today? It's a holiday everywhere.'

'Mom, I have my targets to achieve, and most of the other guys are on leave today, so I'll have to go to office,' I replied.

'Forget about targets, you are working very hard anyway. Don't go today!' Mom insisted.

'Maa, we have to apply for a leave two days in advance. I can't take a leave suddenly like that,' I pleaded.

Mom kept silent. I now wished that I could have done what she wanted. We reached home and I started getting ready for office. Mom requested me to take leave again, but I don't know what happened to me or why I wanted to go to work so badly.

Mothers love their children so much that they somehow feel ominous before something terrible is about to happen to them.

Before I left for office, mom again said, 'I had to go to the temple with you in the evening, how will I go alone?'

But I contradicted her suggestion again and replied, 'I'll take you to the temple when I come back.'

I sat in the cab, opened the window and gave mom a flying kiss before leaving. I wondered why mom was feeling so uneasy. I wasn't able to understand her feelings, which I regret even today.

I reached office. This was the first time it looked so empty. Hardly two or three people were there, all boys. Most of them were those who came by their own means of transport. Rest everyone was on leave. Looking at the office, I thought, 'Why didn't I listen to mom and take a leave today?'

Since I was already there at office, I decided to work. I realized that day how annoying it is to work in an empty office. With what difficulty the time passed that day, only I know. I felt like talking to mom and put my hand in my pocket to take my mobile out, but it was not there. I searched another pocket and eventually all the pockets of my jeans, but I found nothing. I went to the main hall and dialled my number from the office landline. I got tensed thinking that I had lost it somewhere. It rang three times and then mom picked it up. I finally felt relaxed as everything was safe and alright. Mom shouted at me for having left the mobile at home. She instructed me to call her right before retiring from work.

I was the only one who required a cab, so the cab driver was very careless and not on time as usual. I went out of the office to look for the cab. I requested the gatekeeper to call him up as it was already 10 and I had to reach home as soon as. The gatekeeper called him up and told me that the cab would be there in a minute.

Vishnu bhaiya, our cab driver, had left the job a few days ago and a new driver had joined in his place. He was so weird and unmannered that nobody preferred talking to him. I was a little afraid of being the only one in the cab with him. I waited for a few more minutes before my cab finally appeared. As I hopped into the cab, I smelled something weird. It was stinking in there. I later recognize the smell, it was liquor. I asked the driver, 'Bhaiya, what kind of a foul smell is this?'

He retorted and said, 'Nothing, Mehak!'

I cringed. How did he know my name? I felt ominous. He was driving a little rashly and was singing blatantly. I shouted and said, 'Can you please drive slowly?'

'Nothing will happen to you, Mehak,' he deliberately replied.

I got offended as he had called me by my name again. How dare a driver call me by my name, and that too so rudely? I shouted, 'Stop calling me Mehak!'

He turned, smiled shamelessly and replied, 'Isn't that your name?'

I noticed that he had taken a different route. I sensed that something was wrong and admonished him while stammering, 'Where are you going? This is not the route to my place.'

He lied, 'We're going to the petrol pump.'

The road he had taken was empty and dark. I was terrified, so I started praying to god to keep me safe. I thought it better to not panic and think smartly. I started waiting for the right moment to see someone on the road, so that I could shout for help.

He slowed the car at one point and said, 'Mehak, you are so attractive, I couldn't stop staring at you when I first saw you!'

I shrieked at him, 'I will call the police, drop me home quickly.'

'I want you, Mehak,' he replied under the strong influence of liquor.

The thought of jumping from the cab came to my mind, but it was speeding and I would have gotten injured seriously, had I jumped. He finally stopped the car at a secluded place and jumped to the back seat of the cab. He then held my hands. I resisted and shouted, jabbed his stomach with full force and his head hit to the window. Meanwhile, I got some time to jump onto the front seat. I spotted a pen on the dashboard and thought of using it as a weapon. I quickly took it and powerfully jabbed his face with it. He screamed in pain and fell back. I hastily opened the cab's gate and started running at full speed. The road was empty and dark. I was afraid as hell, but I continuously convinced myself to be strong. I was running in the same direction from which we had come.

I recalled my father's instructions regarding noting everything when going to a different place with unknown people and to be alert at all times. That advice helped me remember the way back that day. I ran for approximately 3 kilometres before I spotted a petrol pump. I reached the pump and fell down there, shouting for help. The workers there came running towards me. I told them everything, gave them my home's number and fainted.

Re-Birth

I opened my eyes and saw mom. I hugged her as tightly as possible and cried. She kissed me on my forehead and said, 'Don't worry, beta, you are safe. I am here.'

'Mom, I should have listened to your advice!'

'Forget it, beta, and take rest,' she suggested.

'Mom, who brought me home? I remember nothing. You know what happened? That driver...' Suddenly, mom stopped me and said, 'I know, beta. The police caught that driver.'

'What happened to that driver?' I asked curiously.

'He got what he deserved. Don't think about that incident now and take rest.' Mom gave me a glass of juice.

I tried to sleep, but the whole event flashed in my mind. I felt incredibly impure and started crying. I covered my face with the bed sheet so mom wouldn't notice. I was so disturbed that I felt guilty. I was blaming myself for that incident and for not obeying mom's advice.

When Mohit and Nupur came to know of the incident, they expressed their anger and condolence for what had happened. They also promised to be extra careful in recruiting drivers in future and told us of the new policy that 'no girl will be picked first or dropped last from now on'. 'We will make sure that a male employee always gets picked up first and is always dropped last, to ensure safety for girls,' they promised.

I woke up shouting in the middle of the night. I was dreaming about that incident and felt a little claustrophobic. Mom came running to me and screamed, 'What happened, beta?'

I was sweating profusely. I replied slowly, 'Nothing mom, just a bad dream, don't worry, you go and take rest.'

For the next ten days or so, I continuously woke up in the middle of the night, screaming. I was feeling mutilated. I was not able to attend office since the day that incident had happened. My confidence was shattered and I started feeling afraid of even going outside. I developed an intense hatred for men. I started believing that every man is like that. I found myself angry all the time.

Finally, when I showed no signs of improvement, mom took me to the doctor, a psychiatrist precisely. The doctor asked me a few questions about that incident and about the symptoms. He suggested some anxiety relief therapy with some essential anti-depressants. We started the medication and therapy sessions, which proved to be effective in time.

It had been a month since that traumatizing incident. I was much better. I gradually forgot that event and those malicious dreams stopped haunting me during night. Mom sensed that I had lost my confidence, so she suggested that I start going back to work, as that would help me in regaining my lost poise. I was very reluctant initially, as I was not at all sure if I could do the job, but after Mom's regular insistence, I joined my office again.

The first day was a real struggle for me, I had no idea what to do. I found myself just studying the brochures. I had forgotten all the things which I had learned previously, like product descriptions, sales script, etc. Nupur realized that I was facing difficulty, so she specially requested a new trainer, Karthik, to take care of me. For the next few days, he was to help me regain my lost confidence and sell products.

He was a stout guy with a height of 6 feet. He was hardly 22 years old and had recently completed his education. He had excellent communication and interpersonal skills, so he got hired by our company to train the new people in sales. Nupur introduced me to him saying that I was very good in sales and had an enormous amount of confidence. She also told him that due to some reason, I had not been well for the last month, so I needed the training to regain my lost confidence. I was just standing there and listening to their conversation. I felt terrible that I had become a burden and everybody had to put in extra effort to bring me back on the same track.

When Nupur left, he smiled at me and introduced himself.

He stretched his hand out for a handshake and said, 'Hi Mehak, I am Karthik!'

'Do I look like a ghost? Why do you look so stunned?' He winked and laughed loudly.

I couldn't resist laughing and replied, 'No, it's nothing like that, sir.'

'Ohhhh I got it. Now you want to say that I am very old, I got it now!' he sniggered again.

I looked at him confused and replied, 'No, I don't.'

'You do. You just said 'Sir'. Do I look so old that you call me Sir? Just call me Karthik!' He smiled.

What a sense of humour, going far above from my head, I thought. I gave him a fake smile and replied, 'Okay!'

He then said, 'I have an hour daily for you. Let's hope that I can help you with your problem.'

For the next 15 days, he helped me with communication. He drafted me a good script for calling. We used to practice by talking to each other. He would become the customer and I would call him and give him the product description and all. He gave me many tips regarding excellent communication skills. He always encouraged me to do good and often gave me inspirational examples of successful people who went through some tough time during their life. I never told him about that incident, nor did he ask me. He eventually became like my teacher who guided me through life's little things. He helped me overcome my hatred for men, or rather my thinking that all men are wicked and want something, one way or the other, from women.

I was very impressed with his vast knowledge and sincerity for his work. He was a true professional with immense attitude. He seemed different from the other boys I had met or seen so far. He never talked insensibly, nor did he ever try to start talking about topics that were irrelevant to our work. His focus was always on his work and his responsibility to make me a sound saleswoman.

Mom was pleased to see the kind of improvement I was showing. I often used to tell mom about the teachings he gave me. One day while making dinner, I was talking to mom and telling her about office. I told her that I had recently sold seven products and everyone at office was amazed to see the dramatic improvement I was showing. Mom smiled and said, 'All the credit for this goes to Karthik, he fetched my daughter back.'

I agreed with Mom; he had a kind of magic in him which did a kind of magic on me. My session usually started from 4 o'clock, so I always tried to reach a little early to spend some time with him. This was the first time in my life I was feeling anything like that. I felt closer to him with every passing day. I tried to understand this attraction that I was feeling towards him, but couldn't make sense of it, nor could I talk to anybody about it. I spent my days thinking about him and finding ways to talk to him.

It was like any other day. For the last 15 days or so, my main motivation for going to the office was just to attend the session with Karthik. That day, unfortunately, I got a little late, so I was in a hurry to reach office as soon as possible. As my cab finally entered the campus, I ran in like a small school kid, which reminded me of my school days when Paa used to come to pick me up. I used to run out like that after the last period got over, and tried to reach Paa as quickly as I could.

I entered the conference room breathing heavily due to all the running. Karthik laughed and said, 'We got a new PT Usha here in our office, what's your fastest speed by the way?'

'Very funny,' I replied while trying to control my breathing.

'So, what are we going to do today?' he asked.

'Whatever you want!' I replied.

'Today is our last session. Tomorrow onwards, you are on your own.' He nudged me and winked.

'What?' I replied with a sad face.

'Yes, do you want to get training your entire life?' he asked curiously.

'When I first met you,' he continued confidently, 'I could easily sense that you don't have any problems. It was just your mental block which I had to clear, and see, you are now confident enough to sell even the Taj Mahal to anyone!'

I gave him a fake smile and replied, 'Thanks!'

I asked him, 'Do you want to know what happened to me that broke my confidence and trust in this society?'

He whispered slowly, 'One should forget the bad memories.'

He then towered over me and said, 'Let me give you the last lesson which I learned over a period of time.'

That is a small story that I can never forget.

***

The Professor began his class by holding up a glass with some water in it. He asked the students, 'How much do you think this glass weighs?'

'50 grams…100 grams…125 grams…' the students answered.

'I don't know unless I weigh it,' said the professor. 'But, my question is: What would happen if I hold it up like this for a few minutes?'

'Nothing,' the students said.

'Okay, what would happen if I hold it up like this for an hour?' the professor asked.

'Your arm would begin to ache,' said one of the students.

'You're right, now what would happen if I held it for a day?'

'Your arm could go numb; you might have severe muscle stress or paralysis, you might have to go to the hospital for sure!'

'Very good!'

But during all this, did the weight of the glass change?' asked the professor.

'No!' was the answer.

'Then what caused the arm ache and the muscle stress?'

The students were puzzled.

'What should I do now to come out of the pain?' asked the professor again.

'Put the glass down!' said one of the students.

'Exactly!' said the professor.

Life's problems are something like this.

Hold it for a few minutes in your head and they seem okay.

Think of them for a long time and they begin to ache.

Hold it even longer and they begin to paralyze you. You will not be able to do anything.

It's important to think of the challenges or problems in your life, but EVEN MORE IMPORTANT is to 'PUT THEM DOWN' at the end of every day before you go to sleep...

That way, you are not stressed, you wake up fresh and strong every day and can handle any issue or any challenge that comes your way!

So, when you start your day from now onwards, remember to 'PUT THE GLASS DOWN!'

This story gave me a lesson which brought a significant change in me.

***

My session ended and with that, along with it my motivation to come to office as well. However, I managed to convince myself that I could still see him at office at times and talk to him. I spent sleepless nights thinking about him. I tried to do everything to divert my mind, but nothing seemed helpful.

Despite all my efforts, I couldn't keep him away from my mind and he moved closer to me every day.

After a lot of mental juggling. I concluded that I was in love. But how the hell did I fall in love, I wondered. I tried to hold back my feelings for Karthik for the next few days, but as a result of that, I returned to the same condition that I was coming from. I always found myself immersed in thoughts, I would hardly speak or smile. All I thought about was Karthik and the time I had spent with him. Finally, one day, I decided to let him know my feelings. I thought this would at least help me reduce my soreness. I decided that if he said no, I will not shed a single tear, nor will I become sad. It was not his problem that I love him, it was entirely mine, and if I liked him, it doesn't guarantee that he would love me too.

I bought a card for him, carefully choosing the matter written inside, to efficiently communicate my feelings to him. I wanted to express my feelings to Karthik on some extraordinary day. So I chose Karthik's birthday for this particular thing. Two days before his birthday, I requested Karthik to have lunch with me on his birthday, or rather forced him to give me a lunch party, so that he would be alone with me. Initially, he was a bit reluctant and said that he would give a party to the whole office, but I convinced him to have lunch with me alone and then proceed to party with the office.

At last, the awaited day arrived. I found myself very nervous since the morning itself. I was not sure how I was going to tell him how much I loved him. I was not sure how he would react to a girl proposing. I did not want to look like a minx, but I had decided that whatever he thought of it, it would be his perception. It was essential for me to express my feelings either way. Now it was high time; I would have burst, had I keep these feelings in my heart for one more day.

I reached office and went to wish Karthik straight-away, but he was busy with a training session. I waved my hand and asked him to come out. He shook his head in return which meant, 'I am busy, talk to you later.' I again waved and stared at him angrily, and he came out at last. I shouted, 'Happy birthday, Karthik!'

He smiled and replied, 'Thanks!'

'Let's go for lunch, I am so terribly hungry,' I quickly replied.

'Give me 15 minutes please; let me finish this class,' he said and went back in.

I had already taken permission from Nupur for this. I had lied to her saying that I had some personal errand to run. After about 10 minutes, I texted Karthik, 'I am waiting for you outside the office, come soon.'

To which he replied, 'I am coming soon, don't want to get killed on my birthday.'

A smile came to my face. A few minutes later, I saw Karthik coming out from the office. He came to me and said, 'Let's go for the treat. By the way, where do you want to go for lunch?'

I felt delighted being with him. I smiled and said, 'Wherever you want, Sir. By the way, you are the host, not me. You decide!'

'What about Amar Punjabi?' he asked.

'Sure it's a great restaurant,' I quickly replied.

We took the auto and left. I didn't know much about Karthik. He had never told anyone about his personal life, about his family or where he stayed. On my way to the restaurant, I asked him, 'You never talk about anything apart from the professional stuff, why is that?'

He replied, 'It's nothing like that, Mehak. What should one talk about at office?'

'Yes, that's true. Anyway, tell me about you.'

'Why are you interviewing me on my birthday?' he got stupefied and replied.

'Come on, I want to know!' I shrugged and asked.

'Okay, I don't have any other option, I guess,' he guffawed.

He told me that he stayed in Talwandi with his father, mother and a younger sister. He had done his studies from Kota itself. He had just graduated with a degree in engineering a few months back from Kota Engineering College. His father worked at a private firm called DCM. His mother was a teacher at a government school, and his sister was pursuing a degree in engineering from Delhi.

I was a little surprised to see him working in Kota. He was so knowledgeable and smart that he could easily have gotten a good job at any metro city he wanted, but I didn't ask because he might have taken it the wrong way.

After spending 25 minutes in the auto, we finally reached 'Amar Punjabi'. It was a weekday afternoon, so it was very sparsely crowd. We went to the first floor and took a table at the left corner of the hall. I was shaking due to anxiety, thinking how I should start the topic, how to tell him what I felt. Whenever I tried to speak, some interruption happened, like the waiter arriving, or his phone ringing, while sometimes he got busy receiving wishes from his friends. After about half an hour, I determined myself to speak, but I still found myself struggling to say something. Finally, after an hour, I controlled myself and asked, 'Do you have a girlfriend, Karthik?'

He looked at me confused and replied, 'No!'

I felt relaxed and thought, 'Thank God, he is single.'

I closed my eyes, took a deep breath and whispered, 'Karthik, I love you very much!'

He stopped eating and looked straight into my eyes. He could easily see my eyes full of tears which I was ready to shed in a few seconds. He replied politely, 'Mehak, that's so sweet of you to think, but sometimes the other part of the story is a little complicated and I am sure you don't want to know that. My request to you is to please forget all this as soon as you can.' He had said all this so politely and with so much pain in his words.

I didn't understand what exactly he had wanted to communicate, but I could understand that he wanted me to forget him and my feelings for him, which I couldn't do at any cost.

I again said, 'Karthik, without you I would still be in the same condition that I had been in. I was able to overcome my problems only with your help. It's like God sent you for me. You are different from everyone else, Karthik, you have got a pure heart. You always helped me and made sure that I am fine. I still remember those days when you did everything you could to bring back my lost confidence. I had become a maniac, even after the doctors had quit, you never thought of leaving me in that condition.' Suddenly, my eyes let go of those tears which they had been carrying for the last few minutes.

He silently listened to everything and replied, 'Mehak, please try to understand. I did nothing, I just tried to tell you my experiences and some of the good things which I learned from my parents, especially from my father. I only helped you to forget that incident, but it was your hard work and your dedication which brought back the real Mehak. If I were not there, some other person would have been. Please, don't waste your time on me.'

I wanted to slap him for this last line.

I shouted, 'Don't waste time on you!? You don't know what you're worth, Karthik. Any woman who gets to have you as her husband will be lucky because you are different from others!'

'No one will get me, Mehak. Don't worry about that,' he stammered and replied.

His words got me bemused. 'No one will get you?' I asked. 'Please Karthik, I love you. I have been trying to tell you this for a while, but I didn't know how you would react. Please Karthik, I will die without you!' I pleaded.

He shouted angrily at me in response, 'Don't you ever dare to say die in front of me, okay? You will never understand what the value of life is!'

I had no idea what he was talking about. I just told him that I would die out of fury, I was not dying in reality. His talk was making no sense to me. I had told him that I loved him and he had replied saying that he was not worth it.

'Do you love someone else?' I asked.

'No!'

'Then why are you saying no to me?'

'Mehak, I like you too, but...' he stopped in between. 'If someone loves me, it's only a suffering for her!' he completed his sentence after a minute's pause.

I was simply sitting there with no clue. He then said, 'Today is not the right day to discuss all this, I request you, please. We'll discuss this some other day.'

I am not sure, but I think I saw tears in his eyes. I felt the pain in his request and changed the topic. I smiled and said, 'Okay, okay please, don't be sad. See, I brought something for you!' and gave him the card and a wallet which I had bought for him.

He opened the gift wrapper, saw the wallet and smiled. He still looked sad to me though. He then saw the card which said, 'To the most wonderful boy I have ever met!'

He stood up, hugged me and left. I was astonished by his weird behaviour. He came back in 10 minutes. I could see that his eyes were red. I wondered if he was crying. I asked him, 'Where were you?'

'In the washroom,' he replied.

I asked, 'Do you want to order any dessert?'

He replied, 'No, it's fine, let's leave. I have a lot of work at the office.' We took an auto and left. On our way back to the office, we were quiet the entire time. I didn't know what to say, I was confused by his answers. I wanted to know why he had given me such weird answers, but I didn't want to upset him again, so I didn't ask.

I was so agitated that I wasn't able to sleep all night. I was confused as he had neither said no, nor yes. The only thing he did was give me weird answers. I wanted to know desperately what he was hiding, so I decided to ask him about it the next day. That night when I slept, I saw a dream in which I was with Karthik and we were walking hand in hand as a couple.

'Karthik, I want to talk to you. Could you please come out for 1 minute?' I texted him when I reached office the next morning.

'Not now, Mehak. I am in a session. Let's talk late in the evening,' I got the reply.

'Why is he ignoring me? There is definitely something which he is hiding,' I thought.

I could hardly concentrate on my work, restlessly waiting to talk to Karthik. I saw my watch. It was showing 8 o'clock. I texted him again, 'Can we talk now, please?'

'Okay, coming out in 10 minutes,' he replied.

After 10 minutes, I saw him coming out from the main gate of the office. I was very nervous as I was going to say I love you again, and it was the second time in two days. I wondered how many times I would have to repeat the same thing to him. He asked, 'Yes, tell me, what do you want to talk about?'

'I want to say that I love you!'

'Not again, Mehak. I told you yesterday also. I am not born for this kind of a thing!' he gave me a weird answer again.

I shouted indignantly, 'What kind of weird replies are you giving me? If you love somebody else, just tell me directly. I will not utter a single word after that.'

'There's nothing like that, Mehak. It's just...' He paused.

'If there's something you want to share, I'll be glad to hear it, Karthik. You are not getting my point. I am feeling like this for the first time in my life, it's a bizarre feeling for me. You'll always be in my thoughts. I can't live without you. Just say yes, please!' I started crying.

'I don't know whether you know this or not. I too like you very much, you are a nice girl. When I first saw you helpless and depressed, I heard a sound in my head, like someone was telling me to help you and bring you back to life. You are very different from other girls and I will be lucky to have someone like you in my life. But-' He stopped again.

'But what?' I shouted

'Promise me, you won't tell this to anyone!' he requested.

I was baffled, because I didn't know what he wanted to say and replied, 'I promise.'

'I have Leukaemia. I am here only for the next couple of months, at most a year, if lucky.' He smiled with a few tears in his eyes.

I looked at him and said, 'If this is a joke, I am telling you, I will give you a tight slap, Karthik.'

'Do I look like I am joking? I know the value of life. That is why I shouted at you yesterday when you said you would die. I want to live more, Mehak, but this fucking disease of mine won't let me live!'

I felt like someone had jabbed me hard in the stomach, I could feel my legs shivering. I suddenly became dumb. My inner self started chanting Krishna's name, I closed my eyes and collapsed. I couldn't feel my legs, it was as if they were not a part of my body. Karthik held me and helped me stand. In my mind, I was shouting at God for having done this to Karthik. How could it be possible? He looked so fresh, so young, and so full of energy. He never even took leaves due to a fever, then how could it be possible that he had Leukaemia? My mind didn't want to believe in all that shit. I thought that maybe he was lying just to get rid of me.

I stood there so shocked that I wasn't even able to react in any way. At last when I looked into Karthik's eyes, I burst into tears. He tried to stop me from crying, but I still continued to cry for the next half an hour. When I finally stopped crying because I did not have a single tear left, Karthik held my hands and said, 'See, that is why I didn't want to tell you this, I don't like people crying for me.'

After hearing that, all I could do was hug him tight and cry again. I felt like I was in some form of trauma. He politely said, 'Please don't cry, Mehak. It's not up to any of us anymore. When I first came to know about this, I cried a lot too. Gradually however, I came to accept the truth and now I am happy. Before I told you this, did you even imagine that I could be suffering from a deadly disease? I hope not, because I hardly think about it myself. I have decided to live out every breath left in me to its fullest. My whole family has also accepted that I'll not be around soon. It's not like we didn't try for a cure. My body requires blood once in every 15 days. Doctors are trying, but in India, Leukaemia still kills thousands of people. That is the only reason why I didn't go out for jobs. We first discovered that I am suffering from Leukaemia when I was in 1st year. One day, I suddenly collapsed and when I came back to my senses, I was informed that I was going to die in the next 4 or 5 years.'

I was standing there helpless, listening to him. I was so in love with him that if God had come to me and asked me to take his diseases, I would have done that too. I held Karthik's hand and said, 'You are mistaken if you think that after hearing this, I will stop loving you. If I had just a day left to live and God asked me who I wanted to spend it with, I would want that day to be with you. I love you that much, Karthik. I want to be with you no matter how many days you have or I have, and please, don't you ever dare to say that you are not born for love. You deserve everything which anyone else in this world deserves!'

'Mehak, please try to understand. The day I came to know about this disease, I decided not to ever fall in love with anybody. Falling in love amplifies your desire to live, which would make it all the more difficult for me to die. Mehak, believe me, I don't want to die in vain. I want to die happily without the fear of leaving someone shattered,' he replied insistently.

'You are wrong, Karthik. Love gives you satisfaction and contentment. I still love you, Karthik, and I can confidently say that I love you more now,' I said, looking straight into Karthik's eyes and went into the office.

A few minutes later, my phone rang and I saw a message from Karthik which said, 'Mehak, for the first time in my life I felt that God did something good to me by sending you to me. I love you too!'

I smiled and shouted like a small kid who had just got his favourite video game set. I laughed gleefully when I noticed everyone staring at me. I said sorry and sat back to read Karthik's message again.

Being In Love Is Like Being In Heaven

'Eyes, let's go for dinner today,' I texted Karthik, or 'Eyes', which was the new name I had given him.

'Okay, Sweetu. I will see you at office. I love you,' he replied. Now I had become his Sweetu, and he, my Eyes.

A month had passed since he admitted that he loved me. Being with him was like being in heaven. We were madly in love with each other and I was so pleased about that. Everybody in office now knew that we were committed, and everyone used to tease us with the other's name.

I used to pray for his health daily as his health was very unpredictable. We used to meet in the office every day and sometimes for dinners and lunches too. I was thrilled to be with him, but soon this happiness was going to end as my 12th standard exams were going to start in a few months and as promised to mom, I had to leave the job. One day, we were sitting in a garden. I was despondent because I was going to resign from the office in a week. Karthik somehow sensed my sadness and asked, 'What's the matter, Sweetu?'

'Nothing, just feeling sad,' I replied.

'For resigning?' he asked with a confused face.

'How will we meet, Eyes? I will miss you!'

'Sweetu, you and I are connected by our hearts. We don't require meetings to love each other. I will also miss you, sweetheart, but at this point of time, your priority should be your studies. I may not be here always, but your education will be with you forever.'

I kept my hand on his lips to stop him from talking like that and said, 'Why do you always remind me of that, do you like it when I cry?'

'No baby, it's a reality you can't run from. It is better to just accept it and do your studies and make me feel proud of my Sweetu,' he nudged me.

'I will, Eyes. I promise you that, but this whole week I want to spend with you so that after I resign, I can study effectively.'

'We will meet at office anyway, Sweetu. What's the matter?'

'No, not at office. Let's not go to office for the next one week,' I winked.

'What? Are you kidding me? It's not possible, Mehak. I have important training sessions,' he retorted.

'No, I am not kidding. In fact, I have a better plan. Let's go out somewhere. I'll tell mom that our whole office is going out for four days. What do you say?'

'Are you crazy, Mehak? Let me give you one advice. Never lie to your parents, they are the best friends anyone can ever get, and if you have to lie to them about something, then you probably shouldn't do that thing at all,' he replied indignantly.

That was the reason why I loved him the most. Whenever I was about to do something wrong or even think about it, he ushered me towards the right way, never supporting me in my crazy ideas. He said that I was immature and didn't know the difference between right and wrong.

'Okay, let's drop the outing plan, but can we please spend time in Kota together?' I asked, fuming.

'Of course, Sweetu. You don't have to take my permission for this,' he chuckled.

Mutually, we decided to take leave for seven days to spend some quality time together, which would have enabled me to study thoroughly after I resigned. We also decided to apply for the leave the next day itself.

'What excuse will I give Nupur?' I asked Karthik.

He smiled and replied, 'That is what I was about to ask you. What excuse should I give to Mohit sir?'

I laughed and replied, 'See, even our hearts are attached to each other and think alike when required!' and we both burst into laughter.

Finally, we decided that I would give an excuse of my relative's wedding and he would give an explanation of his uncle's house warming in Delhi. We were very confident that we would get leaves with these excuses, but sometimes, life plans something else for you.

The next day, the first thing we did when we reached office was to apply for leave. First, I went to Nupur and asked for the leave and got it approved fortunately. I messaged Karthik, 'Eyes, I got the approval, yeeeeeee.'

'I am going to Mohit Sir's cabin. Let's see what happens,' he replied.

Fifteen minutes later, he came to my desk with a bemused face. I asked him, 'What happened?'

'I told Mohit sir that I am going to Delhi for the inauguration of my uncle's house so I would need leave for seven days. He asked me if I knew Vaibhav from HR. I told him that I did. He said they are all planning to go to his wedding in Delhi and that I should join them.'

I screamed, 'What the hell! How could this happen?' Karthik and I knew Vaibhav very well. I was surprised why Vaibhav hadn't told us anything about it. We would have planned something else if I had known.

'Now, what should we do?' I screamed at Karthik.

'Nothing, just come to Delhi. Now you don't have to lie to your Mom. Let's go to Delhi,' he guffawed.

The next day, I went to Nupur and said, 'Ma'am, yesterday after I asked you for leave, I got to know that Vaibhav is getting married.'

'Yes, we all are going, but you will miss the fun as you have another wedding to attend,' she replied

I quickly said, 'Ma'am, Vaibhav is a good friend of mine. So I have planned to attend my relative's wedding on Monday and Tuesday, and then I would come to Delhi. He would get angry if I don't come.'

'Okay, that will be great!' she smiled.

As soon as I came out, I called Karthik and said, 'Eyes, listen, as per Nupur, I am attending my relatives wedding on Monday and Tuesday, so I'll not come to office on those days. You better take leave for two days so that we can spend some time in Kota, and then we will go to Delhi together. Isn't that exciting?'

'Yes it is, now I will have to ask Mohit Sir for a leave on Monday and Tuesday as well,' he replied.

'If you don't want to meet, just tell me. Don't make a sad face,' I shouted and cut the phone.

A few minutes later, I received a message from Karthik, 'I would die a 100 times just to spend a minute with you.'

A tear rolled down from my eye and I replied, 'Don't even dare to use the word die in front of me again and sorry for being so rude, I love you!'

'Okay, I'll not, but promise me that you will never get angry with me,' he replied.

I smiled and replied, 'Eyes, you can't even imagine how much I love you. How can I be angry with you? I promise, I won't, but only if you be with me always.'

He didn't reply. I waited for his message for the next few hours. Later, I understood why he hadn't answered. In these few days, I had forgotten that he had cancer, but he remembered.

Since the day I had joined office, I hardly spent any quality time with my family. Also, the next day was Sunday, so I decided to make up for it. When we were having dinner, I asked Maa, 'Sahil and Khushboo hardly go out. Tomorrow is Sunday, so let's go out somewhere and have fun. You are always so busy with the mess too, this way you can also change your routine.'

Mom replied, 'It's a good idea, let's go out tomorrow!' I was very excited, so I left the dinner in between and went to Sahil and Khushboo. They were busy fighting with each other. When I told them about the next day's plan, they started shouting and singing out of joy. We decided to go to the 'Traffic Garden'.

Later that day, when we reached back home after our little outing, I was helping mom clean the utensils when she asked me, 'How is Saurav? Is he also going to Delhi?'

I was hearing his name after a long time, so I was shocked. I replied, 'He left the job a few months ago.'

'He was a nice guy!' Mom replied while scrubbing a plate.

I changed the topic and said, 'Maa, today we enjoyed ourselves after a long time. We should go out like this every week.'

'Yes, after such a long time I went out and saw the world. Otherwise, all I usually see is the mess.'

'Don't worry, Maa, once I finish my graduation and get a good job, you won't have to work anymore. I won't let you!'

'Beta, you are a girl and you will have to get married after you graduate. After you are married, I will have to take care of Sahil and Khushboo too.'

'Maa, I will never leave you. I will keep you, Sahil and Khushboo with me after my marriage, I promise,' I replied with a stern face.

Mom smiled and replied, 'How can I stay with you after your marriage? Anyway, let's leave it to the future. You have to go to office tomorrow, so take rest.'

When mom used the word 'marriage' I felt a different kind of a sensation and Karthik's face came to my mind. I imagined him in a white and golden groom's clothes and he looked very handsome. Suddenly, I started to feel a little different about Karthik. Now, he was more than a friend, boyfriend, or mentor. I wanted to be with him for the rest of my life. I stopped myself from thinking that way as I wasn't sure how long he was going to be with me.

***

Except me, everyone else in the class decided to go to school for the coming one week. I had to go to Delhi, so I could go only for the next two days. While I was at school, I heard my classmates planning for the board exams. I got severely tensed as I hadn't even started thinking about reviews. I promised that I would study seriously once I came back from Delhi and make paa proud of me.

After school, I reached home. I was officially on leave that day, so there was no cab sent for me. I got ready and told mom that for the next two days I would have to go to office on my own as our cab driver was on leave. Although Karthik had told me to never lie to mom, but it was the only solution at that time. Otherwise, mom would have asked so many questions. We had decided to meet at the Radha-Krishna temple in Talwandi, so I took an auto and went there. I reached there on time, but couldn't find him so I messaged him, 'Where are you, Eyes? I am waiting for you outside the temple.'

Instead of his reply, he came in front of me and said, 'I am here at your service, madam. What can I do for you?'

'Yes, let's go inside and pray,' I held his hand and took him into the temple.

'Radha Krishna' temple was and will be my most favourite temple in Kota. The statue of Krishna in the temple is so beautiful and well-crafted, that it seems as if Krishna himself is standing there and giving his blessings to you.

I stood in front of the beautiful statue of 'Radha Krishna'. I closed my eyes and prayed for the happiness of my family. I was mesmerized by the beauty of Krishna that I started singing a bhajan in my mind. Before I left, I prayed for a long life for Karthik too. I held Karthik's hand and we took seven rounds around Krishna's statue. It felt as if we were doing 'Fere' and it felt perfect.

We came out and sat in the garden opposite the temple. I asked, 'Eyes, what's the plan? Where are we going?'

'I don't have any plan. I thought you would have some plan, like always,' he winked.

'You have decided that you will never make any plans? Do I always have to do it?' I asked with a bemused face.

'I didn't say that, yaar. Accha, I'll make a plan for today, okay? Let me think,' he replied. 'Let's go for a movie!' he exclaimed.

'Eyes, I want to spend time you. How will we talk inside the theatre?' I stared at him.

'Yes, you are right. Let's go to the gurudwara in Badgaon then, I have wanted to go there for a long time,' he replied excitedly.

'We will go there, but not today. Tomorrow maybe,' I said reluctantly.

'See, that is why I don't make any plans because you never do what I plan. Tell me, what should we do today?' he asked with an irritated face.

'Eyes, I love you. See, the weather is so good today. It will probably rain, let's go boating,' I nudged him.

'At last, we always do what you want, so what is the use of me making plans anyway?' he sniggered.

I smiled and said, 'You and I are one, so what's the difference, Eyes?'

He held my hand and smilingly replied, 'Nautanki, let's go for boating.'

Karthik had borrowed a bike from one of his friends, so we didn't have to search for an auto that day. He started the

Pulsar, and we proceeded towards 'Chambal garden'. It was a weekday, so very few people were there. I mostly saw couples there who must have bunked their classes and come there to spend some time in privacy. That is what we were doing there as well, the only difference was that I had bunked my office.

We took the entry tickets for the garden and went in. The climate was splendid, cool breeze was flowing. Sun was peeking gently from behind the clouds, and the tall coconut trees in the garden added five stars to the beauty of the park. I felt like I was at some hill station, looking and admiring the natural beauty there. The aura there was so astonishing that one could quickly fall in love with that place.

We were holding each other's hands and enjoying the beauty. I felt a strong urge to express my love for Karthik, or perhaps it was the environment which was provoking me to do so. I held his hand more tightly. He looked at me and I quietly spoke, 'Eyes, promise me one thing?' He saw me impishly and asked, 'Yes, Sweetu?'

'I want to marry you,' I replied.

He looked straight into my eyes and said, 'Sweetu, I want to be with you always and forever. I can't imagine my life without you. I can promise you one thing though, I'll always be with you, whether I am alive or dead. As far as marriage is concerned, Sweetu, we are connected by our hearts, we don't need a name for our relation. Our relation is so pure, like water, and I am so thankful to God that he gave me a ray of happiness in the form of you. Perhaps God was happy with me or took pity on me, I don't know. One thing is for certain that he has given me a prized possession which I cannot afford to lose.' A few tears rolled down from his eyes.

'I won't let anyone take you away from me, not even God,' I cried.

He held me by my shoulders and said, 'I also wanted to tell you something.'

'What?' I asked.

'Promise me that you won't react badly after,' he quietly replied.

'Tell me quickly, yaar. I'll not, I promise.' I couldn't handle so much suspense, especially when it concerned Kartik.

'I had my check up in Fortis a few days back, and got my reports the day before yesterday. My cancer has gotten worse, despite having taken all the necessary therapies. Doctors suggested us to consult the Boston Cancer Hospital which is the only hospital in the world that can treat my cancer. They have all the essential treatments required to treat a case like mine,' he said in a shaky voice.

I didn't know how to react. I didn't know if I was happy that he was going to Boston for treatment, or sad that his cancer had gotten worse. I was confused and was thinking about how to react, but my heart reacted faster than my mind and I found my eyes shedding a few tears. I was standing in a numb position when I heard Karthik's voice, 'Sweetu, don't be upset. I'll be fine. Boston Cancer Hospital is the best in the world. I'll come back from Boston fit and fine, and then I promise, we will get married.'

Still immersed in my thoughts, I heard the word 'marriage' and came back to my senses. I replied, 'What did you just say?'

'I said, I'll come back fit and fine from there, and then I promise I will marry you,' he repeated nervously.

For the first time, Karthik was feeling positive about his treatment and I could easily judge that from his voice. I didn't want to have him think negatively again, so I smiled and replied, 'I'll miss you, Eyes. I can't live without you,' and hugged him tightly and cried.

'It is an expensive affair though, Mehak. In fact, being from a middle-class family, it seems quite unaffordable to us. But...' he stopped.

'But, what?'

'But my father wants to try every possible treatment, so he wants to sell our house and arrange the money for the treatment,' he said with a sad face.

I was speechless, seeing his father's love for him. I was proud of his father. I inquisitively replied, 'Why are you sad, Karthik? He loves you and he doesn't want to quit trying. I am proud of your father.'

'Our house is the only property we have and I don't want my father to sell it for me, that too for something we are not a hundred percent sure will work,' he said.

'Karthik, try to see this from your father's perspective. House is just a material thing. How can you even compare it to yourself? You are far more important for him than your house. When you get fine, you can buy many houses like that.'

'Let's see what happens,' he replied.

'When are you planning to go, by the way?' I asked.

'The preparations and formalities will take another month or so,' he replied.

I hugged him and said, 'Please be in front of my eyes as much as possible.'

'I want one more promise from you,' he replied.

I confusedly asked, 'What promise?'

He held my hands and replied, 'Promise me, you will never let my disease affect your studies and your life. Promise me that you'll be happy always and even if I die, you'll remember me with a happy face and never with tears in your eyes or with a sad face. Please promise me all these things and swear on me.'

I didn't have any option, so I promised him all the things that he said, but I asked Karthik to spend the next five days with me happily and not think too much about the future.

After that, we went to the boating area. We took the tickets and waited for our turn. At last, we sat in the boat with five other guys. As soon as the boat started, I felt little water drops on my hands and soon it started to rain which made the activity of boating all the more interesting. I also got a little afraid and grabbed Karthik's hand tightly. He looked at me, smiled and said, 'Boating was your idea, madam. Now don't be afraid.' The scenery from the moving boat looked great. On either side of our boat, there was a rocky terrain, which made me wonder how such a place had survived in the middle of our city.

After about ten minutes in the boat, the water didn't scare me as much anymore, so I put my hand in the water and splashed it at Karthik. I was having fun. Karthik told me not to do it, but soon joined me too and started throwing water at me.

When we got off the boat. I ran after Karthik and was shouting, 'Come here, I'll show you how to play Holi.'

He was running too and said, 'You started it, I didn't.' Suddenly, he stopped and sat on a bench, he was breathing heavily, as if he had just run a marathon. He told me that he was feeling dizzy and wanted water. I ran to the nearest shop and bought a water bottle. He was still breathing heavily when I gave him the water. After about fifteen minutes, he became normal again. For the first time I realized that his disease was killing him from the inside, he had become weak and could not run for more than a few meters. I became anxious for him. I was holding his hands tight and felt aghast. He realized that I was getting frightened, so he smiled and said, 'Don't worry, I'll be out of this misery soon.'

I rested my head on his shoulder and replied, 'I know, Eyes.'

'Now, what next?' I asked Karthik. 'Let's go to Karai ke Balaji,' he said excitedly.

'Which place is that?' I replied.

***

We reached the main gate of 'Karai ke Balaji' in about five minutes. It was very close to the boating place. From the front, I could only see the small gate behind which the river Chambal was flowing in full flow. I got excited to see the place and quickly went in. The place was located on the banks of the river Chambal, and the whole area was built on top of rocks, so the floor was all rocky and uneven. As I entered from the left side, I saw a small temple, outside of which there was a group of swans running here and there. For the first time in my life I was looking at live swans. They looked so beautiful and white. There were around 15 swans there; some of them were sitting, while some of them were eating. I was busy contemplating the beauty of swans when Karthik shouted, 'The main attraction of this place is downstairs.'

'What? There is something downstairs too?' I exclaimed.

'Yes, Sweetu. Come on, I'll show you,' he smiled and pulled me while holding my hand.

There were stairs on the opposite side of the temple, made from cutting the rocks. I went down the stairs and when I saw the view from there, I felt as if I was hypnotized. I simply stood and looked at that place dumbstruck.

On the left side, there was a small temple of 'Shiva'. The beauty of the temple was that the water of Chambal river touched the stairs of the temple, so there was water everywhere on the floor. I had never been to a river beach before, so I was mesmerized by the beauty of that place. The main attraction was on the right side of the stairs, where there was a big rock on which I saw many guys sitting and enjoying the weather. We sat on it too and I took off my shoes and dipped my feet in the cool water below. One of the boats in the river was the same boat in which we had been rowing a few minutes ago. I smiled at Karthik and said, 'Eyes, thanks for bringing me here. This place is superb.'

I somehow fell in love with that place. I promised myself that I would return to that place with Karthik again. We stayed there for another hour or so, but we didn't say a word because we were too beholden with the exquisite beauty of the place.

'I am feeling hungry,' Karthik said, looking towards a flower basket in the river.

I looked at my watch. It was 7 o'clock already. I replied, 'Let's go for dinner,' even though I didn't want to leave that place. We went back to where he had kept his bike and he said, 'Where for dinner?'

I replied, 'You tell me.'

'Not again, Mehak. Tell me quickly, or I will collapse due to starvation,' he said.

I wanted to tease him, so I replied, 'Are you sure you want to do what I say?'

'Yes, Mehak. You know I don't have an option,' he replied smiling.

'Great, then let's do something weird. Let's go to somebody's reception and crash the party.'

Karthik suddenly stopped the bike, turned his head towards me and said, 'I had a doubt about your mental state before, but now I can say for sure that you are crazy.'

I laughed loudly and replied, 'You look so cute when you talk like this. But let's try it once and see how it feels.'

'Mehak, please don't try to convince me to do this. If someone catches us, it will be very humiliating,' he said with an endearing face.

'Areee, no one will notice, yaar. There are so many people at a reception, who all will they observe. Besides, we are both well dressed today so no one will even be suspicious.'

I don't know what had happened to me that day, I was acting entirely different. One could hardly tell that it was the same Mehak who was once an introverted and timid kind of a person. Even I couldn't believe what I was asking Karthik to do. After convincing Karthik for the next 10 minutes, he gave up and agreed, as if the kid inside him had taken over the charge and now wanted to do something notorious.

After roaming for about 20 minutes, we finally found a reception underway, near the Airport road. By the number of vehicles parked outside, we could guesstimate that there were a lot of people there. Karthik said to me, 'Mehak, let's not do this. This is not fun.'

'Come on, Karthik, it will be fun. We will not eat for free. We'll give money. Look at this envelop I have here.' I took out an envelope from my purse and put a Rs. 100 note in it.

Karthik knew that he had to do what I wanted, so he didn't resist anymore and said, 'Let's go, but if someone notices that we are not related to either the bride or the groom and insults us, don't blame me, okay?'

'Yes. sir. Let's eat now, I am hungry,' I winked.

As we entered through the giant gate decorated with flowers and lights, we saw a huge ground covered in red and black carpet. On the left side, there was a stage on which the groom and bride were sitting. A lot of people had gathered around them and were congratulating them. We were starving, so we went to the food area. I didn't want to look at the ground, but I also didn't want to look into anyone's eyes. I was in fear of arousing suspicion. I was feeling strange about it all. It was Karthik who was acting like a professional wedding crasher instead. He greeted everyone, even laughed with a few people. Thankfully, we reached the dinner area without anyone noticing anything amiss about us.

We picked up the plates and reached the stalls. People there were in queue loading one dish upon another on their plates. We also lined up behind them. The food looked delicious so we quickly picked as many dishes as we could and started eating. While eating, I teased Karthik by calling him 'you thief' and laughing. Karthik stared at me and replied, 'Don't tease me, Mehak.'

We thoroughly enjoyed ourselves and ate as much as we could. The free food seemed to have increased our appetite. We finished our dinner and I looked at Karthik and said, 'Let's go and give our wishes to the bride and groom.' We went up to the stage, acting like we had been invited to this wedding and had known the couple for a long time. I wished the couple a happy marriage and a great life ahead and gave them the envelope. They were looking at us strangely. I knew what they wanted to ask, 'Do we know you?' but they didn't as it would have been rude. Their role was to quietly accept the gifts from the attendees, and that's what they did. We climbed down the stage and Karthik said, 'Let's go.'

I didn't know what happened to me, but I said, 'Hey, we didn't taste the desserts. I want to have some ice cream. Let's eat ice cream quickly and leave.'

'Not again,' Karthik screamed. I held his hand and took him over to the ice cream section. I asked the waiter to give me the chocolate flavour one. Suddenly, I heard someone say, 'Mehak, what are you doing here?'

I recognised the voice but I closed my eyes in fear and prayed to be proven wrong and for it to be somebody else. I stood like a rock, not daring to turn back and see who she was. I heard the same voice again, 'Mehak, I am asking you something.'

I turned around reluctantly and saw Mom standing there with Sahil and Khushboo. I was dumbstruck and didn't know what to say. My mind was working as fast as it could, thinking of so many excuses at the same time. I replied stammeringly, 'Mom, I am here with my colleagues. How come you are here?'

'The bride lives in the neighbourhood of our mess and often comes there too. She insisted a lot that I come to her wedding. I told you yesterday about the wedding, didn't I?' she asked.

I was even more confused than Maa, so I replied, 'No.'

'Perhaps I forgot. Kids wanted to go outside for dinner, so I brought them here and prepared food for you at home. I thought we'll be back by nine before you came home. But look, what a surprise, my daughter is here herself,' she said.

'Ohhhh, shit!' I shouted in my mind. I remembered the invitation card I had seen on the table. I cursed myself for not looking through it properly and ending up in front of Mom with Karthik. Karthik, I suddenly remembered that Karthik was there too. I looked around and saw Karthik standing far away from me and laughing. I stared at him angrily, but it seemed as if he was enjoying my situation. I knew mom would ask me a few more questions.

'How do you know the couple?' she asked, as expected. This was a tough question to answer.

I knew that if I lied and mom ever got to know the truth later, I would be in big trouble. I decided to say something which was more diplomatic than a straightforward lie. I replied, 'The groom is a good friend of my boss, so he asked my boss to come here with his entire team.'

Mom then asked, 'Where is your boss and your colleagues?'

'Ummm, actually we were about to leave when I saw you, so I told them to leave as I could go home with you.' I was stammering throughout.

My mom was no less than James Bond 007, so she said, 'You didn't see me, I saw you.'

'Arey Maa, I saw you first, but I wanted to eat the ice cream, so I thought of getting it first and then come to you. Now come on, let's go home. I am tired.' I changed the topic and took Sahil in my lap.

Finally, mom quit and we went back home. I was feeling so relaxed that everything had gone okay and mom didn't see me with Karthik. It could have been a big problem. I wondered why Karthik was laughing so much, it was not a comical situation. Or was it? When we reached home, I went straight to bed to avoid any more questions by mom. I messaged Karthik, 'Tumhe to beta kal dekhti hun main, BTW, I am missing you, Eyes.'

When I woke up in the morning and checked my cell, I saw Karthik's reply, 'Miss u 2, Sweetu. C you tomorrow.'

That day, as we had decided, we met at 'Radha Krishna' mandir again. As soon as Karthik looked at me, he started laughing like a maniac. When he didn't stop laughing for the next few minutes, I too couldn't control myself and started laughing too. At last, Karthik said, 'I can't believe this, Mehak. Your mom was there. Too good.'

'I was shivering like anything when I heard mom's voice. Seriously, it was very shocking,' I chuckled.

'So, what's the plan today?' Karthik winked.

'We decided yesterday, didn't we? Let's go to Badgaon,' I replied.

'Okay, but for God's sake. don't do anything adventurous today,' Karthik replied sarcastically.

We reached Badgaon in an hour. The place was so divine and so pure that one could automatically become pure just by entering the temple. The temple was made up of white marbles. There was a different kind of harmony there. We went in and said our prayers. A beautiful hymn was playing there, though I couldn't understand it as I didn't know Punjabi, but it was very soothing. When we were coming out, the priests there told us to take the prashad, also called Bhandara in Punjabi. He ushered us towards the hall next to the temple. As we entered the hall, we saw hundreds of people eating there. We wondered when and how so many people came there, as we hadn't seen many vehicles outside the temple. I got tensed again because I did not want anyone to see me with Karthik again. Karthik somehow guessed my thoughts, nudged me and said, 'You wait for me outside, I'll go in there and bring the prashad.'

I quickly replied, 'Yes, that's a good idea.'

Karthik came outside in a few minutes with a plate of food, I saw the plate and said, 'You went in there to bring the Prashad or to get food for the entire neighbourhood?'

Karthik chuckled and replied, 'That guy gave me a plate full of food. Come on, let's eat.'

'What should we do next?' I said while taking in the last bite of the delicious halwa.

'Can't you sit idle for some time? Why do you have to do something all the time?' Karthik winked.

'Stop teasing me,' I smiling.

'Okay, angry young woman. All ready for you Delhi tour, Sweetu?' Karthik kissed my hand and asked.

'Ready? I just need to pack and come, that's it!' I replied.

He sighed.

'What?' I asked in a confused manner.

'Sweetu, people always go shop when they go out for events like this, but you never do any shopping. It's strange.'

'Those people are rich and have lots of money to spend on those stupid things, I don't.' I replied with a smile.

Karthik hugged me and said, 'You know one thing, Sweetu? You are 1000 times better than those people in all aspects. You deserve the best, you are my angel and will always be.'

Before I could reply, Karthik shouted in joy and said, 'Let's go shopping today, I don't have any good clothes to wear at the wedding.'

'Good idea, let's go,' I replied.

In Kota, there were usually no good options to shop at, so we went to Gumanpura - the hub of garments shops. Karthik parked his bike at a central location so we could cover all the shops on foot. I ushered him towards a garments shop and said, 'Look at those mannequins in suits, they look good. Let's go in there and see some nice suits for you.'

Karthik smiled and ushered me towards a shop on the opposite side of the suit shop and replied, 'Look at those dummies in such nice salwar suits. Let's go in there and look for some nice suits for you.'

'We are here to do shopping for you, not for me, buddhu,' I said while laughing at his spontaneous answer.

'No, we are here to shop for you, Sweetu, not for me. I have enough clothes. If I had told you to do shopping for yourself, you would never have come here, so this was my trick. Now come on, let's go and get something nice for you.' He held my hand and took me to the shop forcefully.

The salesman showed us a few salwar suits. Out of sheer habit, I first looked at the price tag and rejecting those that were too costly. I didn't want to let Karthik notice it, so I told the salesman to show me some different colours, but the salesman was a duffer and kept showing clothes in the same price range. When Karthik finally understood what I was trying to do, he said with a sad face, 'Sweetu, do I mean anything to you at all or am I somebody whom you can't take anything from?'

I didn't know how to reply, so I preferred to keep silent. He picked up a nice cherry coloured suit which I had liked in the first glance, but rejected due to its high price and asked, 'Do you like this?'

I nodded my head, still without saying anything. Karthik told the salesman to pack the suit. He paid him Rs. 900 and we came out of the shop. I was not able to say anything, nor did I want to because I usually avoided spending someone else's money. I had always believed that it's nice and satisfactory to spend the money you earn, and it was almost painful for me to use someone else's hard earned money for myself.

When Karthik asked me why I was being so silent, I told him what I thought. He held my hands and said, 'After I die, what will I do with the money I have earned? I will feel good if you have something gifted by me.'

I shouted and pleaded him to shut up. I hated it when he talked about dying. I angrily said, 'You go to Boston and better return well, and this is the last time I am warning you not to say anything like that. Don't you ever dare talk of your death like this again.'

'Sorry, Sweetu. It's just that sometimes I have to blackmail you emotionally,' Karthik touched his ears.

'This was mental torture, not emotional blackmail!' I said angrily.

'Sorry, now let's go and buy a matching pair of stilettos also. Come on,' he nudged me forward.

I didn't want to get blackmailed again so I did what he asked and bought a pair of red stilettos.

In the evening, he dropped me home. As expected, when mom saw the shopping bags in my hand, she was amazed and probably couldn't believe her eyes. I had to convince her that I had changed and was now interested in shopping like any other girl. Mom was also aware that I was going to Delhi to attend my colleague's wedding, which was reason enough to justify the shopping. The next day, we had to reach the office at 10 A.M. so that we could all leave early by a bus arranged for us by our company. I had done my packing the previous night itself to avoid any last minute rush. Mom was worried as usual and gave me many suggestions and instructions to follow.

The next day, I reached office at 9:30 A.M. As per our previous plan, Karthik was to meet us directly in Delhi, since he was supposed to be attending another wedding there. When he reached office, everyone was shocked to see him there. Mohit sir saw him and asked, 'Weren't you supposed to meet us in Delhi, or did I make a mistake in hearing you that day?'

Karthik stammered and replied, 'No, sir. I mean, yes sir. I had to meet you guys in Delhi, but due to some urgent work, my family and I returned to Kota day before yesterday. So I thought, why not go with you guys only.'

I looked at his nervous face and smiled quietly at his situation. We all boarded the bus and reached Delhi in no time, enjoying and singing all night. For the first time in my life, I witnessed a big fat Indian wedding. The bride's father was a prominent businessman in Delhi, so the wedding was no less than a big show of their immense wealth. All the rituals were sophisticatedly planned, with all the small details taken care of by the bride's father.

It was the day before the main wedding night. Karthik and I finally got some spare time to spend with each other. We were standing on the terrace of a nine floor high building that was allotted to all of us for staying. It was no less than a five-star hotel. A cool breeze was blowing. Looking at the dark brown sky, I felt like it was going to rain. I began to shiver as the cool breeze caressed my body, as if showering soft kisses all over it. The aura was titillating. Suddenly, Karthik held my hands and hugged me tightly. I let his body's warmth relax my shivering. My heart started racing due to the closeness of our bodies. My hormones were raging wildly. I wanted to be in his arms for the rest of my life. I hugged him as tightly as I could. I could sense that he was a little nervous. I looked at his face, still holding him firmly. He looked into my eyes and my heart took control over my being. My lips parted to greet his lips and we kissed for the first time. As our tender lips locked with each other, a jolt of electricity passed through my spine. We were lost in kissing each other for what felt like the most beautiful moment of an eternity, when Karthik suddenly took a step back and stopped himself and me from getting carried away with our emotions. I looked at him curiously, my eyes still asking him for more, as I was not nearly satiated with his lips. He smiled at me and said, 'You are the best thing that has happened to me,' and quickly walked away. I stood there motionless for the next few minutes, reliving the best moment of my life.

Leaving The Office

Those three days passed in a jiffy. I was oblivious to everything but Karthik and the immense attraction I felt towards him. I can still confidently say those were the best days of my life.

I was back at home and cherishing those moments while lying on my bed. I knew I had to resign from the office soon, but frankly, I did not want to leave such a lovely place of work at all. I was also aware that I had to study and do something better with my life.

It wasn't just the last day of office, but the last day for me to meet Karthik as well. He was going to leave for Boston very soon and I had made up my mind that I would ask him to make me a promise before he left.

I was lost deep in thought when Mom came and sat next to me. She was aware that I was resigning the next day, so she said, 'I know it's hard for you to resign from the office, beta, but I hope you understand that at this stage, your priorities should be studies.'

I replied quietly, 'I know, mom. Don't worry, I'll study hard and get good marks in the board exams.'

Mom smiled and said, 'I know, beta, you will, but I have been noticing for a few days that you have changed a little bit. You seem to be thinking something all the time. Is there anything you want to share with me?'

I got shocked as I didn't know my behavioural change had been so apparent. I knew I couldn't tell her about my relationship with Karthik, so I replied, 'There is nothing like that, maa. It's just that I have been overthinking about my studies.'

Mom kissed my forehead and replied, 'Don't overthink, beta, just give your 100%.'

***

The next day, when I woke up, I felt a little different. It was weird to leave a place after having made so many friends there. I didn't know how I would tell Nupur that I was quitting. I spent the whole afternoon thinking what would happen when I reach office. That day, I wanted to talk to every person in the office.

While entering from the main gate, I saw our gatekeeper, Mohan Ji. I had never talked to him till date, and the only thing I remembered of him were his salutes. He always saluted everyone when they came in or left. He was a nice man who always smiled and talked positively to everyone, especially girls. For the first time, I saw him properly. He was an old man, probably in his 60's. I don't know what came over me, but I felt a strong desire to go and talk to him. As I entered from the gate, he stood up, saluted and said, 'Good morning, Mehak Ma'am.'

I smiled and said, 'Good Morning, Mohan Ji.'

He looked shocked on hearing me reply, as I had never replied before. I asked him, 'Where do you live, Mohan Ji?'

He replied, 'Ma'am, I live near Tipton. It's a small place near our office.'

He looked happy to be talking to me so I continued, 'How many kids do you have?'

'I have two kids, Madam, and one of them is a CA,' he replied proudly.

Wow, I thought, he is a regular gatekeeper, but his child is doing CA. How wonderful is that! I said, 'That's great, Mohan Ji.'

I could see his eyes welling up with tears and pride for his son. Taking a deep breath, he said, 'Yes, he is a hard working boy. He has cleared his second phase and is preparing for the third. I am sure he will pass that too. I put whatever I have in his studies, and he has proved that he is worth that sacrifice.'

He was a proud father and his eyes were expressing that feeling. He inspired me to do something great too as we were not too rich either. I could easily relate to him.

I was pleased to hear about his son and said, 'Mohan Ji, tell your son I wish him all the best for his studies.'

He quickly replied, 'God is with us, ma'am, and when he is there, what else do I require?'

'I wish him to be with me for my whole life too,' I smiled and left.

I straightaway went to Nupur and said, 'Hello, I want to tell you something.'

Nupur replied, 'Hi Mehak, do you want to see pictures from Vaibhav's wedding?'

I wasn't able to say no to her and said, 'Yes Nupur, sure.'

She called everyone to her desk and for the next half an hour, we all saw the pictures and laughed. One of my colleagues noticed that I was standing near Karthik in almost every picture and he informed everybody of his observation. We became the butt of everyone's jokes too.

When everybody left, I again said, 'Nupur, I want to talk.'

'Yes, tell me, Mehak. What's the matter?'

'My board exams are coming up and I have to prepare for the exams, so I'll have to leave the job,' I said.

Nupur looked up at me and said, 'Yes, exams are important, Mehak. But why leave the job, just take three months' leave.'

She said this very easily and got busy with her work. I didn't know what to reply as she had effortlessly solved my problem, but mom had clearly told me to resign, I thought. I again said, 'But it may take more than three months.'

'No issues, Mehak. You can join whenever you want to, but don't resign. I don't want to lose a good employee like you,' she said without delaying for a second.

I was speechless on hearing that, and I didn't know what more to say, so I said, 'Thanks for having confidence in me, I'll join as soon as I am free from my exams.'

'Sure and all the best for your exams. Prepare well and make us all proud,' she smiled and tapped me on my shoulder.

I went to everybody's cubicle to say goodbye. Almost half the day passed saying goodbye to everyone. My watch showed 7 o'clock. I had already tried Karthik's number twice, but he hadn't answered. I was getting worried, so I decided to try his number again when one of my colleagues came to me and said, 'Mehak, Mohit sir has summoned you to the conference room.'

I disconnected the phone in between and went to see Mohit sir. As I entered the conference room, I saw all my colleagues looking at me. I looked at everyone and spotted Karthik smiling from one corner of the room. I had no idea what was going on when I saw two of my colleagues come in with three big boxes. Mohit sir chuckled and said, 'Mehak, Nupur was telling me that you are taking a break from work to prepare for your exams, so here is your farewell party.'

Karthik opened one box and took out a big cake. I was mesmerized to see a pink cake with 'all the best little master' written on it. Then came the other two boxes filled with pastries and sweets. Mohit sir ushered me towards the cake and asked me to cut it. I was nervous being the centre of attention there, but at the same time it felt good to receive such an overwhelming farewell. I closed my eyes for a second and prayed that everyone should get a company like that to work at.

Everybody started clapping as I cut the cake. Somehow, I controlled my tears and thanked everybody. When everyone went out of the conference room, I stared at Karthik and said, 'Where the hell were you, Eyes? I was so worried.'

He laughed and replied, 'I was preparing for your farewell party.'

'You are so sweet, Eyes,' I smiled and replied.

'And you are such a liar,' he winked.

'I need one promise from you,' I said.

'I'll give you any promise, but right now I have sessions to take. We will talk when I drop you home.'

Before leaving office, I met with everyone once again. As I crossed the main gate, I noticed Mohan Ji saluting me. I went to him and said goodbye and thanked him for all the times that he had shown me respect. He looked at me with his old eyes and saluted again. I don't know what came over me, but I bent down and touched his feet. He looked at me with a shocked countenance and said, 'God will always grace you with his love, beta.' I felt extremely happy taking his blessings. I saw Karthik watching me from a distance. When I reached near him, he said, 'I don't know why, but I want to respect you more and more every day.'

We were on our way home when I said, 'Eyes, I want one promise from you.'

'Anything, Sweetu. Tell me?'

'Promise me, you will meet me once before you go to the U.S.'

I could feel the bike slowing down as soon as I asked him for this promise. He replied, 'That will be sometime during your board exams, most probably.'

I hastily replied, 'So what? I can manage 2 hours, but I can't let you go without meeting me.'

'Promise, Sweetu. I promise we'll meet before I go to the U.S.'

I hugged him tightly from behind and replied, 'Thanks.'

'Okay, but for now, I have something for you,' Karthik chuckled.

'What is it, Eyes? Tell me quickly,' I hurriedly replied.

He stopped his bike in the dark at one side of the road and opened his bag's zip. I looked at the bag inquisitively and wondered what he would take out. He took out a small box wrapped in beautiful paper and said, 'Don't open it now, open it when you reach home.'

I tried to convince him to allow me to open the box right then, but he didn't listen. He dropped me seven houses before mine so that no one would notice, and slyly kissed me goodbye. Mom asked me during dinner about my day and the reaction of my bosses. I told her that they didn't permit me to resign, but gave me four months' leave to prepare for the exams instead. Mom seemed to be a little worried about me joining the same call centre again, but she didn't express her tension.

Before going to bed, I opened my gift, tearing the wrapping paper as fast as I could. When I finally got the box opened, I saw a beautiful little statue of Krishna. I was delighted to see it. Under the statue was a small letter. I opened it full of curiosity. It said, 'Sweetu, all the best for your exams. Keep this statue on your study table and carry it in your bag when you go for your exams. You have to score good marks in the exams so study hard for it; I know you can do it. Don't miss me much because I am always there in your heart with you. I want to meet you once before I leave India. Remember, I love you wherever I am.'

***

I kept the statue on my study table. It was a strange feeling to be at home the entire day. I had developed the habit to be busy all day, so I was wondering how I would manage my routine. After thinking for another 15 minutes, the best idea I came up with was to make a timetable to study.

Karthik and I had decided to talk, but only when I wasn't studying. He was leaving in a month and had to make a lot of preparations. His father was trying to sell their house at a reasonable price so they could arrange money for his treatment. I recalled my conversation with Karthik when he had told me that the total cost of his treatment would be around ten lakhs.

I could imagine the kind of pressures and tensions he and his family were facing. I prayed for everything to be fine and for all their problems to come to an end soon. I wondered why everything depended on money. To study, you need cash; to lead a proper life, you need cash; if you are sick and need treatment, you need cash. Money is everything.

Our mess was going okay, it was making enough money to fulfil our daily needs at least. Mom and I knew, however, that this money would not be enough when Sahil and Khushboo would grow a little older. I didn't even know how I was going to manage the fees for my college. Thus worried and crying, I used to fall asleep every night.

Love Is In The Air

It had been five days since I last talked to Karthik, so I decided to speak to him that day. I didn't know whether it was a heart to heart connection or if he had installed a few cameras in my house, but he knew everything I was doing or even thinking. Before I could call him, he called me. I was pleased to see his name on my mobile screen. I quickly picked up the phone and shouted, 'Hey, Eyes! You won't believe it, I was just thinking of calling you and see, you called.'

He replied, 'I have told you before, my heart can talk to your heart, Sweetu.'

He sounded a little low so I asked him, 'What happened, Eyes? You sound low.'

He told me that the day before his father had sold their house to a property dealer and he was despondent about that. I could hear sobbing sounds from the other side of the call. I said, 'Eyes, don't cry please. If you cry, what will I do? I can't bear you crying. Please stop crying, when you become fine again, you will gift him ten houses like that.'

'I know, Mehak, but how will I make that happen? Sometimes, I wish to God that I would just die quickly.'

'Eyes, listen to me. Why are you talking like that? This is not in anybody's hands, destiny has its own plans. Have faith in God and believe that you'll be fine.'

'Hmmm, I didn't know what happened to me. I used to be a boy who always thought positively, but I just can't stand the fact that my father had to sell our house because of me. Anyway, I called to tell you that I am going to Delhi the day after tomorrow for my VISA interview.'

'Interview?' I replied, confused.

Then he explained the whole process to me, what all you need to do when going to America. It seemed to me a little too difficult to get a U.S. visa. I asked Karthik why they took an interview before issuing a U.S. visa.

'They want to make sure that you will not stay there forever. They get many illegal immigrants who come to the U.S. and don't go back,' Karthik replied.

I wished him all the best and we hung up the phone. I was feeling sorry for Karthik and his family. I didn't know how to help them, but I decided to earn enough money to support my near and dear ones whenever they would need me, so they don't have to sell their houses.

I did not talk to Karthik for the next two days. I was waiting impatiently for his call, wondering whether he got the visa or not. I remembered him telling me that only 50% of the applicants get the visa, the rest get rejected. I waited, but he didn't call.

The next day, the first thing I did was to call Karthik, but he didn't answer. I tried again, and he picked up this time. I quickly asked him about his Visa. He told me that he had got the Visa and that he would call later as he was busy, and hung up. He called me in the evening and informed me that he would have to leave for the U.S. on the 20th of December. Before that, he had to stay in Delhi for the next 15 days for all his check-ups. I wanted to meet him and I was worried about him, so I started crying on the phone. Suddenly, he started singing which automatically made me laugh.

That song was from the movie Taal.

His voice was melodious, I closed my eyes and couldn't open them until he stopped singing. 'That song was dedicated to you and every word was coming out directly from my heart. Now, don't you dare cry, okay, my little master, Mehak?' he laughed.

'Thanks, Karthik, for such a sweet song,' I replied.

'And don't worry, I am not going anywhere without meeting my Sweetu. I already promised you that and you know I never break my promises.'

'I know, Eyes, I'll wait for your call,' I stammered.

'I will call you as soon as I am free. Now please smile, I can't take it when you are sad.'

I smiled and replied, 'I love you, Eyes. Come soon.'

He chuckled and said, 'I am there with you, Sweetu. I love you too,' and disconnected the phone.

The next morning, I got a call from one of my school friends informing me about our pre-boards examination dates. They were scheduled to start from the 2nd of January, which left hardly a month for me to prepare.

From that day onwards, I started studying rigorously for the exams. I made sure that I strictly met my targets as per my time-table. I started getting up at 5 o'clock in the morning to study. I tried to study for at least 6 hours everyday to cover the whole syllabus. One day, Mom suggested that I join a coaching class to avail the guidance of experts during the three remaining months. I didn't want to spend unnecessary money on coaching, but the idea seemed beneficial to me this time as I was facing difficulty in coping with the course.

The next day itself, I asked my classmates about the coaching classes they were taking and found one near my house. That very day I joined there too. In all this, neither did I get a chance to think about Karthik, nor did he call me. One day, I noticed that it had been ten days since we last talked. I left a message, 'How are you, Eyes? I miss you,' but for the next two days, I found myself waiting for his reply.

***

I had been trying to sleep when I remembered that the date was 15th Dec and recalled that Karthik was supposed to have returned that day. I dropped him another message, 'Eyes, call me. I am worried about you.' I had started to get used to messaging him and not getting a reply in return, but this time he was really testing my patience so I decided to call him. His phone turned out to be switched off. I was puzzled but I couldn't do anything besides waiting. When I woke up, I saw a message from Karthik, 'Can we meet today?'

I felt a wave of relaxation wash through me as I saw his message. We decided to meet that evening at our place, the Radha Krishna Mandir. As usual, I reached early and he arrived after 15 minutes. I hugged him in sheer excitement, forgetting that it was a public place. He looked more tired and pale than when I had seen him last. I asked him worriedly, 'Eyes, what happened to you? You look so pale.'

'Nothing, Sweetu. It's just due to the last 15 days.' he replied.

'I missed you, Karthik,' I said with tears in my eyes.

'I missed you too, Mehak. Not a single day passed when I didn't miss you,' he replied affectionately.

'Then why didn't you call or reply to my messages?' I cried and hugged him.

'I was busy, Sweetu. I am sorry,' he replied.

I was caressing his hair when I noticed a little bald patch at the rear of his head. Shocked, I stood up and looked at his head properly. There were no hair at the back of his head. I got tensed and asked, 'What happened to your hair?'

'Nothing, Mehak. I went for a haircut and that idiot barber did that to me,' he stammered.

He had tried to bluff, but I knew no barber could ever do that. I shouted at him and said, 'Karthik, swear to me that everything is fine. Please tell me the truth,' I pleaded.

He paused for a minute and replied, 'I am undergoing a treatment called Chemotherapy, the side-effect of this therapy is hair loss.'

I tried to speak, but I couldn't. I was speechless and confused. I was unaware of the treatment and its side effects. I didn't even want to know, as I couldn't imagine Karthik going through all that pain. He sensed my thoughts. He held my hands and said, 'Sweetu, don't worry. These problems will get resolved in a few months. Doctors from Delhi told me that I'd be fine after getting treatment at the Boston Cancer Hospital.'

I was still quiet. I was only looking at Karthik and praying that his problems would end as soon as possible. After struggling for some time with what and how to speak, I said, 'Go and come back soon, fit and fine. I'll wait for you till my last breath.'

'I will, Mehak. I have something for you, but I want you to open it on 30th December,' he said.

I was puzzled and asked, 'Why on 30th December?'

'I am leaving on the 30th, swear to me that you will open it on the 30th?'

'I promise, Eyes,' I replied.

'Sweetu, I am craving to eat something spicy. In Delhi, all I ate was boiled food, and as far as I know, this is what I will have to eat in the US too. Before leaving, I want to eat all my favourite food,' he said laughing.

I said, 'How can you always be so happy?'

'Sweetu, the day I got to know about this disease, I decided to always be happy and live every moment to its fullest, so that even if I die early, I don't have to feel guilty about wasting my precious time on earth.'

He had made a good point, so I replied, 'You are right, Eyes.' A little smile came to my face.

'I am hungry,' Karthik said again.

I smiled and replied, 'Tell me what you want to eat.'

'Gol gappe and chaat,' he chuckled.

I couldn't control my laughter at his words. I replied, 'Let's go then, Eyes'

We went to Chaupati, the best place for foodies in Kota, especially for junk food lovers. Chaupati was a small place on the main road, with a lot of roadside stalls. As usual, it was very crowded. At every stall, I saw people struggling with each other to place their orders first. Karthik was also trying hard to get his voice heard by the stall guy. Finally, he succeeded. He ordered his favourite, 'Panna Lal's Chaat'. I was looking for a place to sit, but since it was so crowded, I couldn't find any and we used his bike as our dining table. Karthik relished the chaat. As soon as I finished the last bite, I demanded ice cream. Luckily, the next stall was famous for its special Kulfi Faluda. I smiled and had Karthik get me that Kulfi. After gulping it down, I said smilingly, 'I love you, Eyes.'

He smiled and replied, 'I'll miss you, Sweetu.'

My face became sad. Usually, whenever he expressed himself, I became sentimental. Before I said anything this time, he put his hand on my lips and said, 'Miss Senti-queen, I have something for you.'

I stopped him in between and said, 'This time, I have something for you.'

I turned my back towards him and said, 'Eyes, can you please undo my locket for one second.'

It was a locket of Krishna. A few months back, my mother had gone to Mathura where a priest gave her this locket for my safety. I was determined to give that locket to Karthik for his safety.

He took off my locket in a confused state and handed it to me. I then asked him to turn around and face me. He asked, 'What are you doing, Mehak? It's your locket, how can I take this?'

'You and I are one, Eyes. I never considered you separate from me. Our bodies may be two, but our soul is one. Please take this locket,' I insisted.

He quietly wore the locket and asked, 'Why have you given it to me?'

'My Kanha is there in this locket. I have told him to be with you and to bring you back to me as soon as possible.'

He put his right hand on my head and replied, 'I want you for all my seven lives, Mehak.'

I saw a tear in his eyes. I also wanted to cry, but I had decided to not cry in front of him, as that would make him weak. I quickly changed the topic and said, 'Pack warm clothes, Eyes. I have heard the winters are pretty cold there.'

'Yes, I will. Come on, let's go. It's late.'

In the next 20 minutes, we reached near my house where he always dropped me. I hugged him and said, 'I'll wait for you, Eyes.'

'Don't worry, I'll be back in no time, Sweetu,' he smiled.

I stammered and asked, 'Could you please keep me updated about your health?'

'I'll try to call you, don't worry.'

He started his bike and went away. I stayed there and watched him until his bike disappeared around the corner. I felt distressed, but I convinced my heart that he would be fine soon. I reached home and found mom waiting for me, like always. That day she didn't ask me for dinner, as she thought that I was coming from a colleague's birthday party.

I looked at the folded letter which Karthik had given me. I wondered how I would wait for the 30th to open it. I studied for another hour and went to bed. I closed my eyes and desperately tried to sleep, but I couldn't. So many thoughts were coming to my mind; a part of my mind was thinking about my studies, a part was thinking about Karthik's health. I was tensed that I wouldn't be able to solve any of these problems. I wondered when I would be able to decode at least a few of such issues. Never before had I experienced life like I was at that time. As a kid, I had always thought that life was very simple and all things could be got easily. I had constructed my own dream world in which I had everything one could have. What I had come to face however, was so different that all my ideas and thoughts were shattered.

From the next day, I immersed myself completely in my studies. I knew that if I didn't study well, I would probably fail in the exams, which I didn't want. I started studying for 10 hours a day and sometimes even more than that. I was desperately waiting for 30th December to arrive, so I could open the letter that Karthik had given me. Someone has said it correctly, when you keep your mind busy, time flies unawares.

The date was 29th December, and I had finished my dinner and opened my economics book to complete a remaining chapter. My studies were going well. My economics course was about to finish. I started practicing equations and got lost in the world of numericals. When I looked at the watch next, it was already 11:30 PM. I badly wanted to read the letter Karthik had given me and couldn't wait.

As soon as it turned 12, I tore open the letter.

Mehak,

I have always found myself struggling to express my feelings in front of you.

Writing a letter was the only way that I could keep my heart out to you.

I love you immensely, Sweetu. You make me feel important and loved.

I was lonely in my battle with cancer when God sent you to help me overcome my fears. I can't tell you how grateful I am for you, and for all the affection and love you bestowed upon me. When I was first diagnosed with cancer, I cursed God every day for having made my life miserable. I never visited any temples, neither believed in his existence until the day I met you.

I feel lucky to have found someone who loves me the way you do, but it was no less than a miracle to have you to make my remaining days happy and content.

I tried my best to keep you away from me, as I knew I won't be here for too long to love you. I am not sure what you saw in me, Mehak, or why you have started liking me so much.

I love you enough to go bring the moon for you and trust me, I have now started praying to God to give me some more time to continue feeling the warmth of your love.

In a few days, I'll go to the U.S. for my treatment. I swear, I feel confident that I will get better and come back to spend the rest of my life with you. I have never said this before, but I want to marry you and to grow old with you. I feel suffocated without you, my dreams revolve around being with you for eternity. You have regenerated my desire to live more, and I promise I'll come back for you very soon.

Promise me though, if something happens to me, you will move on without shedding a single tear. Instead, I want you to smile whenever you miss me. I want you to study hard and make me and your father proud. Most importantly, I want you to fall in love again. I will feel content if I see you falling in love again.

I want you to be ready for the worst.

I want to share with you a dream I had a few days back.

I saw your friends helping you get ready for your wedding. I saw your face full of happiness and you were blushing too. You were wearing a beautiful red lehenga, and I saw myself in a golden sherwani.

I also saw both of us on a beautifully decorated stage, with our family and friends around. I even heard someone say that we make a beautiful couple.

We were so desperate to exchange the garlands, but your friends lifted you high up in the air, making it impossible for me to put it around you. You then shouted and requested your friends to put you down. We exchanged the garlands and burst into laughter. Our eyes were beaming with happiness. We were both glowing.

I promise you, Sweetu, that we will undoubtedly experience this day once.

I love you more than I love myself.

Always yours,

Karthik

Miles Apart

I used to read that letter almost daily. After a few days, I had memorized nearly every single word, and could have easily narrated the whole letter verbatim, has anyone challenged me to it. My pre-boards drawing closer day by day and the load of completing the course was getting heavier too. Time flew, and the day of my first exam arrived in no time. I was a nervous wreck and didn't know what would happen in the exam. I woke up early to revise my course and scanned through each line of the book like a frantic robot. Before I left home, mom fed me a spoon-full of curd and put a small tika on my forehead. She hugged me and said, 'Don't get nervous, beta. You will do well.'

I was very nervous, but my exam went well. I had answered almost all the questions. I gained some confidence and started revising for the next paper. One day passed after another and and all my reviews went okay. I was now waiting for the result which would tell me where I stood in a class of 42 students. It had been 15 days since Karthik left for the U.S. and I had no idea about his health. Now that I was free from my exams, I began worrying about his health again and wondered if I should call his family or not. I wasn't ready to get another shock in my life. Fate had played so many games with me thus far and I just wasn't up to its machinations anymore. However, I really wanted to know about his health at the same time. After long hours of dallying like this, I finally decided to call his home. A man picked up the phone. I asked timidly, 'Is this Karthik's house?'

He sounded like an old man, as he politely replied, 'Yes, beta. I am his grandfather.'

I stammered, 'I am his colleague from office. I just wanted to know about his health.'

I didn't get any reply for the next few seconds. I confusedly said, 'Hello?'

'Yes, beta ji, I am here. He is not well. His health worsened the day before he had to leave for the U.S.'

'What!' I shouted.

'He suddenly fainted on 29th Dec. We took him to his doctor who said that his body needed blood. They stabilized his condition a little bit and told us to take him to the U.S. as soon as possible, so he left on the 2nd of January,' his grandfather replied. I could easily sense his sadness in his tone.

I disconnected the phone without uttering a single word and a few tears rolled down from my eyes. I fell on the floor in shock. Suddenly, my phone rang and I noticed that the call was from Karthik's home. I picked up the phone and answered uncertainly, 'Uh, hello?'

'Beta ji, I am Karthik's grandfather,' he replied.

I didn't know what to say and was struggling, when I heard him speak again, 'Beta ji, I saw your number on the caller ID and thought of calling you back. I know you are Mehak.'

I was shocked. I asked, 'How did you know it's me?'

'I am Karthik's best friend. He shared everything with me. I know everything about you, Mehak beta. I know you are very concerned about him, but don't worry about him, he'll be fine. You know he loves you very much. The day he got sick, I was with him at the hospital. He told me about the day you proposed to him. Before he met you, he was like any other regular kid, doing a job and going about his life, but he was very alone from inside. He didn't feel any happiness from inside, but you changed him, Mehak, and I want to thank you for that. He felt elated whenever he was with you, and I am sure he'll come back for you. So, hope for the best, he'll be fine.'

All I could say was, 'Thanks, Dadaji.'

He replied, 'I will keep you updated about his health, okay? Now tell me, how were your exams? Karthik told me you had your pre-boards in Jan.'

I was shocked that the old man knew so much about me. I said, 'Exams went fine.'

I felt quite pleasant and relaxed after talking to Karthik's grandfather. Karthik didn't have many other friends, and now I knew why. He had a beautiful friend in his life in the form of his grandfather.

Days passed without any significant events. After the pre-boards, my board exams were upon my head, and I had to really engross myself with its preparation. It was like a season of exams, everybody at home had exams. Khushboo and Sahil were busy with their final exams too. Every student who came to our mess had exams. Studying all day and night was not my thing, I was never a book worm. I couldn't keep reading books for a long period of time. Days were passing by very slowly, and I was desperately waiting for my boards to finish so I could join my job again. Every week, I used to call Karthik's grandfather and inquire about Karthik's health. As per my last call with him, his health had shown significant improvement.

I still remember, the date was 13th February and I was helping mom prepare dinner, when I suddenly felt something terrible inside. It was an awful feeling, like I was not well. I didn't understand it and continued my work. I struggled to study the entire night, but I wasn't able to focus at all. Appalling thoughts kept coming to my mind. I closed my eyes and prayed to God for the safety of all my loved ones. I tried to divert my mind a lot, and even listened to songs when I found myself struggling to study, but that terrible feeling wouldn't go away. I wanted to cry loudly. Suddenly, I saw Karthik's face. I looked at my watch, it showed 11 o'clock. I dialled Karthik's home number as quickly as possible, but no one answered. I was so distressed that I couldn't wait till morning to call, so I called again. Finally, on the second ring, Karthik's grandfather picked up the call. I almost yelled into the speaker, 'Daadu, how's Karthik?'

I heard him sobbing. I shouted again, 'Daadu, please tell me!'

He replied, 'Beta Ji, we lost him a few hours ago.'

I heard Daadu crying like a small kid, I couldn't handle his bawling and disconnected the call. I told myself that he was lying, this couldn't be possible. I was cursing Daadu for such a bad joke. I started acting like a maniac, talking and shouting at myself. I was shouting at God for having put me through such a condition again. I had forgotten that I was at my home. I was crying as if I there was no one else around me. I was so loud that mom came running to my room and asked me what happened. I was not in a condition to tell her anything. I just kept on crying which made her very furious. She shouted and asked me what happened. When I still kept on crying like a mad person, or like someone who had just saw a ghost, she gave me a tight slap and shouted at me to tell her what happened. Mom got so scared to see me in that condition that she started crying too. It took half an hour for me to regain my senses. I then saw that Khushboo and Sahil were there too, looking at me and crying. I hugged mom tightly, and she asked me again, 'Why are you crying?'

I told her everything, from the day I had first met Karthik to the day he died. Mom heard every statement of mine very quietly, without uttering a single word. When she had finally heard the whole story, she didn't shout at me. Rather, she calmed me down and said, 'I understand your situation, beta, but there are some things which are not in our hands. I don't want to see you depressed ever again, Mehak. I'll die if the same thing happens to you again. Please, if you love me, don't loose yourself again. I need your support very much. I don't have anyone to share my pains and worries with, apart from you.'

Mom was saying these kinds of things to me for the first time. I could sense the pain in her voice. I instructed my heart and mind to stop crying in front of mom. I wiped my tears, hugged her and said, 'Mom, I promise, I'll always be there to support you in every way possible. I promise to be strong enough. You are the only person on earth whom I love more than anyone else. Don't worry, I'll be fine. Trust me, mom.'

My heart wanted to cry loudly, even as I was talking to mom. I was shattered. I wanted to go and see Karthik. I wanted to talk to him. I wanted him back somehow, anyhow. I was afraid of expressing my true emotions in front of mom, as I didn't want her to get tensed. Mom and I talked for hours, sharing each and everything with each other. When mom went to sleep, I lay down on the bed and put a blanket over my face so that no one would notice that I was crying. I cried the entire night, not being able to sleep for even a minute.

The first thing I did the next morning was to call Daadu again and ask if I could come and see Karthik's body. I was shocked with the reply I got. He said, 'Beta ji, you remember the letter which Karthik gave you? He gave me a similar one, which he requested me to open in case he died. I was sure that he would come back, so I kept it aside somewhere. Today, I opened that letter and you won't believe what I have found.' Daadu started narrating his message to me.

Dear Daadu,

If you have opened this letter, it means that I am no more in this world. Daadu, I want you to remember that you'll always be my best friend. There are very few things that I am thankful for in this life, and one of those is you. I still remember how you always comforted me when I used to cry, day and night. You stayed up late into the night to tell me stories when I was a small kid.

I want to apologise to you for not being a good grandson, since I will not be able to help you in your old age. Daadu, believe me, I would have fulfilled every demand of yours if I could have, but unfortunately, I am not going to be able to do that.

I want you to narrate this letter to mom, dad & chhoti also.

Dad, you are the best dad any child could ever have. I wish I could stand beside you and take the family's responsibility on my shoulders, like you have been doing for the last 40 years. I am very sorry that you had to sell the house you purchased through sheer hard work and austerity because of me. When I talk to God, I will request him to give me one more chance to repay every single effort you had put in for my treatment. I never wanted to go to the U.S. at the cost of selling our house, but just because you had faith in the doctors there, I went. I wish I could have changed your decision of selling our home.

Maa, I love you so much that I want you to be my mom in every birth. I know I gave you so much pain and suffering. I know you used to cry every night, worrying about my health. I wish I could give you the happiness you deserve. I wanted to earn well and buy you a gold statue of KRISHNA, which you have always desired for the temple in our home. Maa, I want a promise from you. If you want me to be happy, please don't cry. Believe me, when you shed a single tear, I die a hundred deaths by seeing you in pain. I promise you that I'll come back, and from that day onwards, I'll make sure that you never cry. I love you, Maa.

Choti, I hope you'll always remember your promise to me, to become a son to Paa and Maa. I will miss you always. You know, I wanted to give you a big car when you got married, but fate has something else in mind. You have great potential, you can achieve anything you want. I want you to take care of Maa. You've always been a great sister. I cherish the moments we have had together and the games we used to play together as kids. You are the sweetest sister anyone can get.

Daadu, I want you to promise me one one thing. Please request Mehak to not come to our house and see my dead body. She will break down if she sees me in that condition. She is a small girl and life has already given her so many problems. I always wanted to solve all her difficulties, but I didn't have the time for it. I know she will try hard to see me one last time, but please tell her that I want this. I can't even imagine what condition she is in right now. Please comfort her as much as you can.

I will meet you all one day. That's my promise.

Always Yours,

Karthik

***

Till today, I haven't been able to understand why Karthik didn't want me to see him. I was extremely puzzled and confused, but I always obeyed whatever Karthik told me and I had to follow this too. I killed my desire to see him one last time. One thing I knew for certain was that Karthik would always be in my heart, wherever I go and whatever I do. I know he still sees me and blesses me. That is why I didn't want to cry and make him sore. I controlled my tears and kept him safe in my heart.

From that day onwards, I have never cried, even when I missed him. Whenever I miss him, instead of crying, I look towards the sky and say, 'I love you, Eyes.'

A New Beginning

In all of this, I didn't even notice when my board exams began. I knew that I was going to fail because I had hardly studied in the last two months. With the name of God, my mom's blessings and all the studies that I had done in a whole year, I appeared for the board exams.

After my exams finished, mom suggested that I learn how to cook. As per mom, a girl should know how to cook well to keep her husband happy. Whenever mom used some marriage reference like this, Karthik's face flashed in my mind. It was a weird situation to convince my heart not to think about Karthik anymore. I started going to the mess with mom, while she taught me all the good recipes that she knew. Every Sunday, I had to prepare the dishes at the mess, and it is surprising that the students loved my meals more than my mom's. They started asking mom whether she had hired a new cook. I was surprised to know that everyone enjoyed my food so much. In fact, according to mom, we were getting the most customers on Sunday. I was delighted to be helping mom. She too was happy as she finally had somebody she could trust with the cooking.

The date was 5th May and it was like any other day. I was getting ready in the morning to go to the mess, mom was being a little lazy that day, so I said, 'Mom, we'll get late, get ready quickly.'

Mom said in a low tone, 'Beta, I am not feeling well today.'

I got a little tensed as I was hearing mom say these words for the first time. I kept my hand on mom's head and replied, 'Let me bring some juice for you.'

I went to the kitchen to get some juice for her, but by the time I came back, she had already fallen asleep. So I tried to wake her up to ask her to sleep after drinking her juice.

Mom didn't respond, so I tried to wake her up again by touching her shoulder. She did not move. I got frightened and yelled, 'Mom, get up!' After trying for a few minutes, I realized that she must have fainted. I was so shocked that I didn't understand what to do initially. I ran to my phone and started thinking of whom to call. I remembered Sameer uncle who lived in a neighbouring house. Mom had said that I should call him in the event of an emergency. I quickly scrolled through my phone book and dialled the number listed under Sameer. As soon as someone picked up the phone on the other end, I started shouting without asking who it was on the other end. 'Uncle, please come quickly. Mom fainted suddenly, I have to take her to the hospital.' As I was saying this, I realized that I could have called an ambulance too, so I hung up in the middle and dialled 101 for an ambulance.

In a few minutes, an ambulance arrived. Mom was not moving at all. I asked the paramedics in the ambulance what had happened to her. They said they were not sure and that they needed to do a complete check-up. We reached the hospital in 15 minutes, and the doctors took mom into the ICU. I was not prepared for any shock, so I prayed to God not to do it with me again. The doctors kept mom under observation for a day. The only thing they told me was that there was some problem with her nervous system. They used some medical jargon to describe her condition, but I couldn't make any sense of it. After one day, the doctors allowed us to see her, but before I went in, a doctor called me and explained her condition to me. According to the him, my mom had just survived a nervous breakdown. I thought that it was great news that she was recovering, but the very next moment he told me that the right part of her body had suffered from paralysis, and she could hardly do anything on her own.

Khushboo and Sahil didn't understand what the doctor had just told me, and they kept on asking, 'Didi, what happened to Maa?' I wanted to cry, but there was no one there to give me their shoulder to cry on. In fact, I had to be strong to take care of my brother and sister.

Mom was sleeping, so we sat near her bed. Sahil shouted, 'Maa, wake up, we have to go home.' Mom opened her eyes. She could hardly speak with the right part of her face paralyzed. I wasn't able to control my tears seeing mom in that condition. I ran out of the room and burst into tears. I hated my life. Everyone I loved was slowly being taken away from me. Then I remembered that I couldn't break down, I had to keep calm and take care of mom's treatment and medicines. I also had to arrange for the money to pay the fees for my brother's and sister's schooling.

I wiped my tears and went back to the room. Sahil was sitting in mom's lap and Khushboo was laughing. It was a strange situation. Mom was talking to both of them. I noticed that she wasn't able to speak properly, but somehow, she was speaking to both of them and was telling them some jokes. I was happy to see them like this. I hadn't expected it, but it was nice to see all my loved ones smiling. I went to the doctor and asked him about the next steps. He told me that the right part of her body was showing very less movement compared to the left part, but if she underwent some physiotherapy, this effect could be minimized. The doctor told me to take her home and asked me to deposit the hospital fees. I asked him, how much. He told me to go to the reception to get the bill. I was very worried as the only savings I had from my job were some 10,000 rupees. I prayed the bill to be less than what I had. I reached the reception and asked the lady to generate room number 24's bill. She looked at her computer and said that my bill had already been paid. My eyes widened in shock in disbelief. I asked, 'Who paid my bill?'

'That we don't know, madam. We did not track the source.'

I was confused. I asked the lady, 'How much was the bill amount?'

'Rs.15,000, Ma'am.'

I was still amazed. While on my way to the second floor to get mom, I saw something unbelievable. Saurav was coming towards me with my mom in a wheelchair. Mom didn't know about anything that had happened between us a few months back, so I reacted normally and asked, 'Hi Saurav, what a pleasant surprise! How come you are here?'

He smiled and said, 'A friend in need, is a friend indeed.'

I didn't want to ask anymore questions in front of mom, so I smiled and said, 'Good to see you.'

We reached home and took mom in. I gave her a glass of juice and told her to take rest. Sahil came to me and said, 'Didi, I am hungry.'

Saurav was also there, so he replied, 'I'll go and bring something.'

I went out with him. Before he started his car, I asked him, 'How did you know that mom is unwell?'

'God wanted me to know it,' he replied while smiling.

I raised my eye-brows in doubt and confusion. He said, 'Check your phone. You dialled my number, perhaps thinking that it was someone else.'

He left, while I quickly took out my phone from my pocket and checked the log. It showed that I had dialled Saurav's number on the 5th of May at 9 o'clock. Instead of dialling Sameer uncle's number, I had dialled Saurav's number, by mistake. I felt angry at myself, but somewhere some part of my heart was happy to see him back. He had helped me for the second time. It was so nice of him, I thought. He came back in a few minutes with food and some fruits; I made a fruit salad for mom and served the food for the rest of us. I fed mom with my hands. She looked at Saurav and said, 'Thank you, beta ji, for all the help.'

Saurav smiled and replied, 'Aunty, you are like my mom, and if a mother is in trouble, it's the duty of a son to take care of her.'

I saw mom smiling and it warmed my heart. I gave mom her medicines and we all left that room to let her sleep. When Saurav was leaving, I couldn't resist thanking him over and over again. I was curious to know what had happened when I called him and asked, 'Saurav, why didn't you tell me when I called you that I had dialled the wrong number?'

'I was shocked when I saw your number flashing on my phone's screen after such a long time. I heard you crying and before I could say something, you disconnected the call.'

I said, 'Saurav, I am sorry. You had to take so much pain because of my call.'

'Mehak, please don't talk like this,' he interrupted me.

'Where were you at that time, by the way?' I asked.

'I was in Delhi for some work,' he replied.

'What! You came from Delhi?'

'Even if I were somewhere far away, I would have come for you, Mehak.'

I didn't want to hurt him so I smiled and said, 'I know, Saurav. I wish everyone gets a friend like you.' I could see so much love in his eyes, but as I had told him earlier, I didn't have any feelings for him and only considered him as my very good friend. He was the kind of friend who is always a delight to have, but he loved me very much, and that was the only reason why I became so uncomfortable seeing him at the hospital.

'Come out from your thoughts, madam,' Saurav said with a smile.

I came to my senses and said, 'Oh sorry. By the way, how much do I owe you, Saurav?'

'I knew you were going to ask this, Mehak. You don't consider me your good friend or what?' he replied angrily.

'It's nothing like that, Saurav. It's just that I don't like to keep debts.'

'Mehak, I'll take my money back, don't worry about that. Believe me, it was my money, not my father's. It was from my own savings.'

'Let me know when you want it back,' I smiled.

'Mehak, can I ask you something?' He paused for a minute and then said, 'I am very concerned about you.'

'And why is that?' I asked.

'Aunty is not well, and Khushboo and Sahil are still kids. How will you manage the expenses?'

I was already worried about this thing. The only way I could come up with was to join my job back, so that's what I told him.

'But do you think that salary will be enough to bear all your family's expenses?' he asked.

'I know it won't be enough, but I don't know what else to do,' I replied.

'We have to find some solution, Mehak. Let me think of something, and you also try to think about it. I know you will find something good.'

When Saurav left and I came back in, I seriously thought about the issue, but couldn't come up with anything. I went to mom's room and sat on the floor next to her bed with my head resting on it. A few minutes later, I realized that mom's hand was caressing my head. I looked up and saw mom looking at me. She asked me, 'What happened, betu?'

I stammered, 'N..nothing Maa, just wanted to be with you, so I came here.'

'I know, beta, that you are worried about money. Don't worry. I have some gold jewellery which we can sell or deposit in the bank for a loan.'

'We'll not touch any of your jewellery, Maa. I'll find some other way,' I quickly replied.

'Meanwhile, you can take out some cash from my account for the expenses.'

'Maa, don't overthink it. Please just take rest,' I replied worryingly. 'I love you, maa,' I said and left.

***

When I woke up the next morning, I prepared food for everyone. I then instructed Khushboo to give medicines to mom. For the first time in my life, I realized how difficult it was for mom to manage everything at home. I knew that I would have to keep a maid to look after mom, but I was also aware that I didn't have the money to afford a maid. I requested Khushboo to take care of mom instead. I knew that Khushboo was a young girl, but she always seemed very mature for her age and I was sure she could manage everything for a few days.

I quickly left home for the mess. It was burning hot outside. I wanted to take an auto, but ended up taking the bus to save some money. I had to handle the mess without mom for the first time, so I prepared my mind for a day full of hard work. I also had to do various odd jobs for the first time, that were required to keep the mess running, like purchasing vegetables. We had a guy who helped mom with the cooking and three waiters to serve the food in the evening. Those waiters also helped mom to pack and deliver the tiffins in the afternoon. I requested the cook to come with me to purchase vegetables from the market.

To my surprise, I saw Saurav standing in front of my mess. I asked him what he was doing there. He told me that he wanted to help me, so he had come to my mess. He offered to help by purchasing vegetables from the market. I asked the cook for the names of the vegetables required, along with their quantities, and noted them down. We went to the market together and brought all the required vegetables. The next task was to start cooking food for the students. Saurav was there the whole time to help me with anything I needed. After I finished preparing the food, I asked him if he wanted any.

'Of course, I am damn hungry,' came the reply.

I served him the food and sat opposite him at the table. He was eating food cooked by me for the first time, and I wanted to see his reaction. He took his first bite and exclaimed, 'Awesome, Mehak! You are such a great cook. For the first time in my life I have tasted such tasty daal.' I was happy that he liked the food. It gave me all the more confidence that I could cook well. After the day drew to a close, he dropped me back home. I was thankful to him for the kind of support he had given me that day.

After that day, time just flew. I didn't even notice how a month was over. It only came to my notice when I had to pay the monthly salaries and calculate our profits. The profits were good. The students had taken a liking to my food. The word got around too, I guess, because we were seeing the highest number of customers ever. With increased profits, I hired a maid for mom. My brother and sister were kids and they had to study too, so it proved to be a good idea. Every month, a physiotherapist visited our home to check on mom's condition. He also suggested some exercises to mom, which were helpful against paralysis.

Meanwhile, I was also waiting for my board results which were going to be announced over the next couple of days. I was praying to God to have just passed. I had so many responsibilities and I was worried I couldn't cope with failure at that point.

Finally, the day arrived. One of my friends from school called me up one morning and told me that the results had just been declared. I was anxious, so I asked her to see my result as well and let me know. I didn't have the guts to go and see it myself. I was not confident at all. I went to a temple instead and prayed. I had my fingers crossed and kept waiting for her to call. Every minute felt like an hour. I was watching the clock now and then and was checking my phone repeatedly for her call. Whenever you wait for something desperately, time seems to come to a standstill, and when you are not, it passes at lightning speed. Mom had been noting my restlessness, so she called me to her and said, 'Beta, you will pass the exams. My heart says so.'

I knew that mom was incapable of thinking anything but positive thoughts for me, but I also knew that it would hardly affect my results. You get marks depending on what you write in exams and as far as I knew, I hadn't written much. At last, she called. Seeing her name on my phone's display filled me with such anxiety that I almost didn't want to answer her call anymore. Finally, when her call was about to disconnect, I picked it up. She yelled, 'Mehak, I got 78%! Yeeeeeee.'

I was least interested in hearing her percentage, so I half-heartedly replied, 'Congratulations, what about me?'

'Oh, sorry. I should have told you your percentage first!' she replied.

Anyone standing close to me at that moment could easily have heard my heart beating. It felt like it would pop out of my chest. She paused for a second and then replied, 'You got 51%.'

In my mind, I shouted, 'Yes! I passed my boards,' but I had to react as if I was not happy with such low grades. I simply replied, 'Okay, thanks.'

In the optimism boosted by her good percentage, she replied, 'Don't worry, Mehak. You can apply for revaluation.'

I thanked her for her advice and disconnected the call. I ran to mom and told her that I had managed to pass my board exams somehow. Mom smilingly replied, 'See? What did I tell you a few minutes ago? I knew you would pass.'

'But I got poor marks,' I sadly said.

'Betu, you went through so many bad situations this year. You worked just because you wanted to help me. Not a single girl your age even thinks of doing what you did. Never consider yourself a loser. You are a champion.'

I felt relaxed after hearing those words from mom. She always gave me so much encouragement and support. Sometimes, I feel that it was her words that kept me going for all those years. That day, I realized that a mother is a girl's best friend. She always supported and trusted me in all kinds of conditions, whether it was joining a job, Karthik or handling the mess.

I was also pleased that I could now concentrate on the mess, rather than worrying about re-appearing in class 12th. The next step was to take admission in a college. I knew that my percentage was not enough to get me into a good college. Besides, there was no way I could leave Kota. I had three dependents under my care. I had the responsibility of my whole family, and I had to work hard to fulfil all their needs and requirements. I quickly got ready and left for the mess. Saurav was there that day too. He had reached the mess before me. When he saw me, he smiled and said, 'Saurav at your service, Madam Ji.'

I burst into laughter and replied, 'Go and clean the mess properly.'

'What? No,' he raised his eyebrow and we both burst into laughter.

I told him my board results and he started dancing with happiness. I wondered how someone could be so happy in someone else's happiness. I was glad that I had a friend with such a pure heart as his.

***

Days passed and I took admission at a Government Girls' College in Kota. The fee of the college was meagre, and so were the facilities and the level of studies there. Most poor girls like me used to take admission there because we had to pay only Rs. 3000 per year as the fee. The best part was that we didn't have to go to college, no lecturers ever came to take the classes. The whole college was like an old historical monument which hardly saw any human movement.

One day, I was working at the mess as usual. I was preparing daal when a girl came in and asked the cook to pack a plate for her. It was 10 o'clock in the morning, and it was going to take us another fifteen minutes to prepare the food, so I requested the girl to wait for some time. Looking at her, it suddenly struck me that I had seen her somewhere before, but I couldn't recall where exactly. I went to the girl and said, 'I think I have seen you somewhere, What's your name?'

She replied suspiciously, 'Pooja.'

The name didn't strike a chord so I looked at her awkwardly for another minute, trying to place her in my mind, but I wasn't able to. Finally, I apologised for having bothered her and returned back to work. However, I couldn't get rid of the feeling that I had seen her before somewhere, so I kept on thinking about it. After about 10 minutes, I recalled that I had seen her sitting in my class at college. I quickly went to her and asked her, 'Do you study at the Government Girls' College by any chance?'

She nodded to say yes. I then told her about the day I saw her and she recalled that she had seen me too. I asked her, 'Where are you going in such a hurry?'

She told me that she was going to college. She had come to study in the city from a little village near Kota, called Ranpur. She lived in a rented room and didn't get enough time to prepare food. I gave her the food packet, thanked her, and she left. Suddenly, an idea came to my mind. I quickly dialed up Saurav and requested him to come to the mess as soon as possible. A few minutes later, he was in front of me.

Idea

I told him of my encounter with Pooja. He confusedly asked, 'So, what's the problem?'

'Stupid, it gave me a good idea.' I continued, 'See, there's no facility for food in our college, not even a single stall for snacks. What if we request the college to permit us to start a food stall there?'

Saurav stared at me and replied, 'That's a good idea, Mehak. You little genius.'

That term 'little genius' reminded me of Karthik and my job. I stopped myself from becoming sad as I didn't have time for it. He said, 'Let's go to your college tomorrow and talk to the Principal.'

The next day, we went to the college. Standing outside the principal's cabin, I saw her name 'Mrs. Sadhna Sharma' written on a nameplate hanging over the door. A few minutes later, a peon ushered us into the room. A few trophies and medals were displayed in a glass rack on one side. Two big photos of Gandhi and Nehru were hanging on the wall behind her. In her loud masculine voice, the Principal asked us, 'Yes? How can I help you?'

I cleared my throat and replied, 'Ma'am, I am a first year student in your college and this is my brother.' I felt Saurav staring at me angrily, but what else could I have said?

I continued, 'Ma'am, I noticed that there's not a single food stall here in our college. So many girls who come here to study from nearby villages face difficulty in getting lunch. They either have to spend time preparing food at home or get it from nearby restaurants.'

'So, what do you want from us? To open a canteen for students?' she asked.

Saurav diplomatically replied, 'Yes Ma'am, but differently. We are here to ask for your permission to open a small canteen within the college.'

She raised her eyes confusedly and asked, 'Why do you guys want to open a canteen here?'

I then took charge and painted the entire picture for her. I told her how my mother owned a mess and how we delivered tiffins to students during lunch time and served food at the mess itself in the evening. She nodded her head and started contemplating. After a few minutes' silence, she replied, 'I hope you know that girls here are not very rich and some of them can't even bear the canteen expenses.'

'I know, Ma'am. I am one of them too. I know how it feels to be poor. Prices would not be an issue, Ma'am. We'll charge the minimum amount possible,' I replied without wasting a second.

'I am not sure how you are going to do that, but I think it's a good idea. I really appreciate your views. At least someone bothered to think like that. Even our government didn't try to see how girls manage in colleges like this one,' she replied thoughtfully.

I replied, 'Ma'am, these girls are the future of the country. We need to take good care of them.'

She smiled and said, 'If you need any help from me, let me know. For now, the only help I can do is to permit you guys to start a canteen here. I will instruct the peons here to vacate a small room for the canteen. Tell me, when do you want to start?'

'From next week,' we both replied at the same time.

'Okay, you will get all the necessary help from the college, this I can assure you,' she smiled.

We thanked her and left. Saurav and I were delighted upon hearing her words. From the first look of her, I had assumed her to be a strict lady, but after that short conversation, I felt sure that she had a pure and soft heart which worried about common people.

I wanted to reveal this news to mom with a pack of sweets. On my way back home, I bought a box of Kaju Katli. I reached home and rushed straight to mom's room. I hugged her and put a Katli in her mouth. Mom asked surprised, 'What happened, beta ji?'

I exclaimed in joy, 'Maa, I am opening a canteen in my college.'

Mom smiled and said, 'My beta has taken her first step towards success,' and gave me another hug.

***

From the very next day, we started calculating the expenses that we would have to incur to establish this canteen. I had around 12000 rupees in my bank account and as per our calculations, we needed Rs. 10,000 to do the initial setup. We made a list of things like oil, vegetables, spices, utensils, etc, that we needed to purchase. The only significant job left was to find a good and honest guy to work there, and two co-workers to assist him. When I considered it, the only man I could think of was Mohan Ji, the gatekeeper from my old office. I asked Saurav about Mohan Ji, and he felt the same about his honesty and good will. We decided to go and talk to Mohan Ji about our offer.

We made our way to our old office. When Mohan Ji saw us, he greeted us the same way as he used to. We thanked him and asked, 'Mohan Ji, we are opening a canteen in my college and we require honest and good people to work there. You are the first person who came to our mind when we were discussing the position.'

Mohan Ji replied, 'I am an old man. How will I manage a canteen?'

'Don't worry, Mohan Ji. It is not a big canteen, so we're sure that you'll be able to manage it. Initially, it is just a small setup that'll serve only snacks,' I said.

Saurav said, 'Tell us the salary you want, we will see what we can do for you.'

Mohan Ji smiled and replied, 'I don't know how this is possible, but just yesterday I resigned from this place. I am fed up of working and just want to rest at home from now on. My son has got a good job now and he wants me to leave this grind of work and sit at home too.'

We became a little sad because we were convinced that Mohan Ji was the right man for the job. At the same time, I was happy for him. I gently replied, 'I am delighted to hear that your son has finally got a good job. He is right, you should take rest now.'

As we turned to leave, Mohan Ji called me back and said, 'I don't know why, but my heart is telling me to be a part of your canteen. So, I have decided that I'll work with you.'

A week passed like a mere hour. We decided to do a little puja at the canteen before inaugurating it. As mom was the head of the family, we decided that she should do the inauguration. When we reached college that day, Sadhna Ma'am took us to the room which she had allotted for the canteen. We saw a few chairs and tables nicely arranged around the room. We were happy to see our first canteen dream finally turning to reality. She then pointed her finger to a corner of the room where a cooler and a fridge were kept. I was very pleased to see that. She told us that she had an extra cooler and refrigerator at home, which she figured could be useful here. I was glad to see the kind of support that she was giving us.

Saurav went to a nearby temple to fetch a priest who could conduct the pooja and other rituals there. At 11 o'clock, we started the pooja. After a few mantras and rituals, the priest broke open a coconut and gave us the Prashad. A few minutes later, Mohan Ji arrived with his two co-workers. Finally, we started preparing the first batch of snacks and in no time, girls started to throng outside our canteen. Every girl present there seemed excited to finally have a canteen inside the college. I was happy that I was somehow able to bring a smile to their faces. Day after day, our sales increased and we started getting demands to introduce some new items to our menu. We had decided to keep our prices very low, which were affordable for all the girls there. Yet, even with those low prices, we managed to reap high profits. Gradually, we noticed that almost every girl in the college bought something or the other from our canteen. We were astonished to see that kind of a response from the girls.

Mohan Ji handled the canteen very well and, as expected, he was an honest man. Finally, after my canteen ran successfully for two months straight, I decided to introduce new items to the menu. After a lot of mental juggling, we decided to add a 'Rajasthani Thali' to our menu. It included Daal, Rice, Chapattis, one kind of vegetable, and pickle. Our cost of preparing a thali was 18 rupees. After assessing our profits, we priced it at 25, which was decidedly less than the market rate.

I handled the mess, while Mohan Ji handled the canteen. This way, everything was managed well. One day, I got a call from Sadhna Ma'am. I was surprised to see her name on my phone's screen. I picked up the phone and said, 'Hello, Ma'am. How are you?'

'I am fine, Mehak. I just wanted to thank you again for your canteen idea. The girls are delighted to have a canteen inside the college,' she replied.

'Ma'am, it came to be possible only with your help and support.'

'It became possible only by your strong determination, Mehak. I have a good news for you. When can you come to meet me?'

'I can come tomorrow,' I said.

Journey Of Becoming An Entrepreneur

The next morning, I reached college at 11 o'clock and went straight to Sadhna Ma'am's office. She ushered me in and told me the 'good news'. 'Yesterday, I was at a committee meeting with all the principals of other government colleges. I told them about your canteen and the feedback we've got from the girls, and guess what, they now want the same thing to be implemented at their colleges also.'

I was dumbstruck. I just sat there smiling, not knowing what to say.

'So, what do you think?' she asked.

'Ma'am, I want to do it, but at this stage, I don't have the extra money to invest in such a project.'

'Take your time. I believe that it's a wonderful opportunity for you to grow your idea. I'll wait for your call,' she replied, her confidence in me reflecting on her face.

I wanted to grow my canteen business, but found myself feeling a little reluctant. I wanted to first consult with mom and Saurav. I called Saurav and asked him to come home in the evening. On the other hand, I was excited and happy to see my work finally giving me some positive returns. I came back home as soon as I could and, as expected, Saurav was already there chatting and laughing with mom. They seemed to be discuss some exciting stuff as mom looked quite happy. As soon as mom saw me, she smiled and said, 'Saurav brought jalebis, do you want some?'

I loved jalebis and Saurav knew it. He looked at me and winked. I couldn't resist myself and took a big bite. Saurav asked me curiously, 'What happened, why did you want to meet so urgently?'

I told mom and Saurav the whole thing. I also told them that I was confused and wanted to consult both of them regarding this first. Mom was thrilled and without wasting another second, she said, 'Beta, this is a golden opportunity, don't let it go.' Saurav showed his support too and said, 'I too think that you should say yes to Ma'am.' I told them that I wanted to grab this opportunity too, but that it needed a high initial investment and I wasn't too sure about the kind of reaction that I would get from other students either.

Mom stopped me in between and said, 'Beta, every project needs some investment, and that investment only brings more returns to you. Don't worry about the money. We will pawn my jewellery for the time being and I know that we will be able to get it back in no time.'

'Mom, your jewellery is worth approximately Rs. 50,000 or more, I don't require that much amount. I hardly require Rs. 25,000 to make things work.'

Saurav interrupted us and said, 'Mehak, you can borrow money from me if you want. Give it back to me whenever you can.'

I already knew that he would be quick to offer me help. At the same time, I also remembered that I already owed him Rs. 15,000, which he had given at the time of my mom's hospitalization. He had already done so much for me and I didn't want to take any more favours from him, so I replied, 'Until I repay your 15000, Saurav, I can't even imagine borrowing more money from you.'

I didn't want to sell mom's jewellery either, so I had to choose one of the available options.

I decided that it was better to use the resources available at home. Before pawning mom's jewellery, I promised myself that I would bring all the jewels back as soon as possible. After a lengthy discussion, it was concluded that I'd say yes to ma'am and start setting up the canteens at different colleges. The next day, the first thing I did was to call ma'am and say yes to her offer. She was happy to hear my answer and advised me to go the different colleges and meet up with the principals personally. She graciously set up my meetings with the principals, and that is all I did over the next few days.

I don't know what it was, but all of them were extremely supportive towards my idea. Some of them even offered financial help. In total, I had to open five canteens, three of them in government colleges and two in government schools. My idea was to start all the canteens at a small scale. I wanted to do it the same way I had done it at my college.

I couldn't manage all the work by myself, so Saurav stepped in and took charge. We divided the work between us. While Saurav took the responsibility to arrange for the necessary things like furniture, groceries, etc., my part of the job was to recruit more guys to work at the canteens and to train the cooks to prepare delicious food. It was not as easy as it sounds, as recruiting good people was the main issue. We had no idea where to look for the right people and were simply shooting arrows in the dark, hoping to hit some target. We finally decided to post an advertisement in the newspaper. The day our advertisement came to print, I started getting numerous enquiry calls for the jobs.

I started interviewing workers. I was shocked to see so many unemployed guys in the city, and all of them ready to work for a meagre amount of Rs. 4000 a month. I was even more shocked to see that a few candidates even had a bachelor's degree, but were ready to work at the canteen. I needed educated candidates to look after the canteen, and two or three guys under them to prepare and serve the food. When I interviewed one of the girls who had a bachelor's degree, I found that there were so many girls and boys like her who were struggling to get a job and earn a livelihood. Her name was Roshni and she needed a job immediately due to some personal reasons, so I hired her to handle one of the canteens. Likewise, I found a few more educated people to handle the other canteens as well. I hired them at 7000 a month and the rest were hired at 4000. That whole recruiting process took a week, and I had only three more days left to start the canteens.

One night, I found myself sitting alone and wondering about my life. There was a day when I had wandered here and there to get a job myself, and here I was one year later, recruiting people for positions at my own venture. Someone has said it right, 'You never know where your destiny is going to take you.' At the same time, I also knew that the canteen business was not my final destination. I needed to do something more money-centric. I wanted to give my family everything that they had ever dreamt off. I didn't want to see Sahil and Khushboo suffer for anything in this world.

I somehow managed to finish all the work on time. The day was Sunday, I got a call from the principal of Government Law College. I picked up the call and said, 'Good morning, sir. I have completed all the required formalities and am ready to start the canteen from Monday.' I expected that he had called to inquire about the status of the canteen, but he had some other thing on his mind. He politely replied, 'Good, Mehak, but my reason for calling you is something else.'

I got confused and asked, 'Yes sir, tell me?'

'Mehak, even since I decided to have a canteen at my college, I have been getting calls from various restaurant owners saying that they are interested too. But just because I have said yes to you, I didn't say yes to anyone else. They are even offering me money for my yes, but you know, I am a man of my words, so I said no right away.'

I could sense him trying to manipulate me with his words. He was asking me very cunningly for a bribe for his yes. When I had met this guy, he had seemed to be a very sincere and thoughtful kind of a person. But I had been wrong about him. I knew what he wanted to say, but I replied, 'That's good, sir, I knew I always had your support.'

He smiled cunningly and replied, 'I am supporting you. That is the only reason why I said no to everyone else. I expect the same kind of support from you too.'

'My support is always with you, sir,' I confidently replied.

'Good to hear that, Mehak. So how much can you give me?' he asked straight-forwardly.

I was in no condition to give anyone any money. In fact, I hardly had sufficient money for my own business. Moreover, my canteen prices were anyhow lower than that of the market. I was offering food at half the market price. There was no way I could have given him a single penny, so I replied, 'Sir, my prices are half as that of the prices at any other restaurant or canteen in Kota. I started these canteens in order to help the students studying in government colleges who are not able to afford good food otherwise. It was never my idea or motivation to earn huge profits from your college. I just want to earn my livelihood through this. I won't be able to support you in this matter, sir.'

As expected, he disconnected the call immediately. When I tried contacting him the next day, I heard his voice instructing somebody to tell me not to come to his office.

That was the first time I experienced corruption first hand. Before this, I had only heard of it on television or read about it in the newspapers. I wondered how somebody could affect the lives of so many students, just to earn a few thousands rupees. Those students were not very rich either. They all belonged to poor or lower middle-class families. I remembered my dad's saying, 'Never do anything unfair with anyone, especially with poor people.'

I felt apprehensive because I didn't want to hear such things from other principals too. Luckily, the other ones were honest enough. I had already hired workers for that canteen, and it was not ethical for me to say no to them now, so I had to adjust them to the other canteens. Even after all such odds, I decided to stay enthusiastic and confident about my goal. I felt very positive that someday my hard work would pay-off. I usually discussed all my problems and worries with Saurav, so I told him about the bribe incident to which he replied, 'You have to be prepared for these things. Everyone is running behind money these days. The only thing you can do is to avoid giving bribes as much as you can.'

At the same time, Saurav also gave me a good idea. He told me that instead of referring to them as canteens, we could give them some names. I liked the idea and started thinking of names for my canteens. After a lot of deliberation, I took mom's suggestion. She wanted to name them Ganga, Yamuna, Sarasvati and Narmada. Everyone liked the names a lot. I names the first canteen at my college, Ganga. We ordered new banners for all the names. I was happy to see my business growing. I always wanted to do the work which gave me satisfaction and I knew I was doing a fair job, I was not cheating anybody. I was using everything fresh and of good quality, be it the vegetables, oils, or other eatables.

A month passed after I started the new canteens. Ganga was running in profit. After all the expenses, including the salaries of workers and the groceries' expenses, I was able to make Rs. 25,000 to 30,000 a month.

At every canteen, I adopted the same strategy that I had followed at Ganga. I started with the snacks, and when I started getting a good response from the students, I introduced the thali system. For the Thali, my main challenge was to teach the cooks how to cook good food. Mom taught me quite a few ways to prepare daal, rice, and the other dishes required for a Thali. On Sundays, I started giving classes to the workers. The venue for those classes was my mess. It took me five Sundays to teach everyone how to cook well.

Mom was also getting better day by day. Her doctors had told her a few exercises which were proving to be really helpful for her. She could now walk on her own and also manage her daily tasks by herself. I was very pleased to see so much improvement in her. I thanked God for curing her, but according to her, it was my dedication and love towards her which had done the trick. One day, when I returned home a little earlier than usual, I saw mom preparing something in the kitchen. Doctors had clearly instructed her not to take any stress, so I went to the kitchen and said, 'Maa, why are you cooking? I brought food from the mess.'

Mom smiled and said, 'I am not cooking food. I am preparing your favorite, Gajar Ka Halwa. You are working so hard, beta. You are not even eating properly these days, so I thought of preparing something tasty for dessert today.'

I quickly replied, 'Maa, but you have to take rest.'

'I am fine, Mehak. In fact, I am thinking of starting working again. I get bored sitting at home all day. I want to help you,' Mom replied.

I didn't want to take any chances with mom's health, so I said, 'We'll go to the doctor and if he says yes, then you can start going to the mess. However, you need to promise me that you will only sit at the reception. You will not do the cooking, you will only handle the accounts. If you are okay with this, only then you can come.'

I had prepared Sarson ka saag at the mess that day and brought some of it home too. All of us sat down to eat together after a long time. The three of them loved the food I had prepared and said that I was the best cook in the world. Mom said that my food had a distinctive flavour to it, something that professional chefs spent their entire lives trying to achieve. I was very happy with their reaction. We were eating the tastiest dessert in the world when mom said 'Where is Saurav? I haven't seen him for the last three days?'

I replied, 'He is fine, busy with his job.'

'I think he loves you,' mom looked at me and said.

I wondered how mom had judged that much. I knew he loved me, but I reacted as if I was unaware of everything. I replied, 'Mom, he is just a good friend.'

'A friend never travels all the way from Delhi by just one call. In fact, that one call was made by mistake too. I can see his love for you in his eyes.'

'Maa, believe me, he is just a friend. And as far as love is concerned, I am not sure if I'll ever feel that again with someone else. At the same time, I am aware of Saurav's value in my life. He helped me at times when I was completely alone and needed support. I value his friendship very much and will always do.'

The next morning, I took a break from work and took mom to the doctor. After a complete check-up, the doctor told me that mom was okay. She was recovering fast, and would soon be perfect. The doctor was shocked to see such improvement in that short a time too. He suggested mom some exercises to bring her numb muscles into action. Mom smiled while looking at me and whispered in my ear, 'Let's start going to the mess from tomorrow.'

I was delighted to see her so fit and happy, and replied, 'Done!' We both burst into laughter. We even forgot that we had been sitting in front of the doctor. The doctor had no idea why we were laughing, but just because we were his clients, he started laughing too. Finally, something good was happening to me. As soon as we came out of the doctor's cabin, I hugged mom and said, 'I am so delighted that you are well. I love you.'

Mom kissed me on my forehead and replied, 'I'll always be with you, my angel. I want to see you reach every height that you aim for, and I want to play with my grandson someday too.'

We reached home, and I started getting ready for work. I had to visit all the canteens as it was the first day of the month, the pay-day for all my employees. I had to distribute the salaries to all the workers. With that, I had to prepare a list of items needed at the various canteens too. From the day I had taken admission in that college, I hardly got a chance to attend the classes. I had only attended five or six classes in the last three months. When I reached Ganga, I saw Mohan Ji shouting at his co-worker. When he saw me, he greeted me and stopped screaming at that guy. I smiled and asked him, 'Why are you shouting at him?'

'Nothing, Mehak madam. This guy asks for leave every other day. We are only three of us here, and when anyone takes a leave, it becomes very hard for the remaining two to manage such a rush!' Mohan Ji exclaimed.

I smiled and asked that guy, 'Why do you want a leave?'

He stammered, 'Madam Ji, some people from my village are coming to my place tomorrow to consider my daughter for marriage.'

That guy hardly seemed to be in his 30's. I asked him, 'What is your daughter's age?'

'16 years,' he replied confusedly.

'Why do you want to marry her off at such a young age?' I retorted.

'In our village, girls get married at this age only. In fact, when I got married, my wife was just 14 years old,' he replied.

'Isn't she studying?'

'She has completed her 10th class, that's enough. Now, it's time for her to take care of her husband.'

I became furious listening to his views. According to him, his daughter was only fit to get married and take care of her husband all her life. The state of his thoughts saddened me. Why did people like him not let their daughters study for as long as they wanted, I wondered. I knew that I couldn't go and change everyone's thinking, but I could change this guy's attitude. I yelled back at him, 'If you want to continue working here, let your daughter study again. I'll talk to the principal of her school, she will help you.'

He looked puzzled. I knew that it was unfair to force my decision on him like that, but that was the only way to convince him to let his daughter study. Also, the fee at the government school was only Rs. 300 a month, which he could easily manage. At the same time, I wondered if he had even that much money to send his daughter to school, since he was a poor man. So I said, 'If you agree to send her to school again, her school fees will be on me.'

I called Choti Maharani Government School's principal and requested her to take in his daughter. She told me to send his daughter to school the next day to complete the formalities. I conveyed the same message to him.

He looked a little convinced with that and replied, 'Okay ma'am, but what about her marriage?'

'You let her study first. When she is above 18 years of age, we will see what to do.'

He quietly nodded his head in a yes and turned. I called him and said, 'You can take leave tomorrow; not for her marriage, but to take her to school.'

I looked at Mohan Ji and said, 'Don't worry, I'll give you another guy to work here.'

Mohan Ji thanked me and handed me the month's earnings from the cash drawer. He then said, 'These are 40 thousand, this month's collection.'

I was making a list of items I needed to purchase when I saw some of my classmates coming into the canteen. One of them was Pooja. Pooja looked at me, smiled, and said, 'You've made my life so much easier, Mehak.'

'And how's that?' I asked.

She told me how she had to get food from outside earlier. It was either too costly, or too unhygienic. She had been facing a lot of trouble with food, but Ganga dhaba had solved it for her.

She took a parcel from Ganga dhaba daily, she said. I was enchanted to hear that. I smiled and replied, 'I am happy that I was able to help you in your studies in some way.'

My canteen especially helped those girls who stayed at rented rooms to study. That was my main purpose behind opening Ganga in the first place. Before leaving college, I went to meet Sadhna Ma'am. A few other professors were there at her office too, including the professors who taught subjects that I had opted for. When she saw me standing outside her office, she called me in. I was a little nervous going in as I hardly went to my classes and feared that all the professors thought of me as a bad student. As I entered, she greeted me and said, 'Nice to see you, Mehak.'

I looked at everyone else present there and replied, 'Same here, ma'am.'

My English professor said, 'The food at Ganga is delicious! Where did you learn such good cooking from?'

I slowly replied, 'From my mother, Ma'am.'

Then, my economics professor said, 'You know, Mehak, the day I ate the food at Ganga, I stopped bringing food from home. I now take my lunch there only.'

I felt sheer pleasure when I heard those comments from the professors, but I didn't want to show my happiness too much, so all I did was just smile at them.

Everyone gave me different compliments for Ganga. Sadhna ma'am quietly heard everyone and then looked at me and said, 'Mehak, you need to ponder over the state of your studies too. I know you have family responsibilities and believe me, you are fulfilling your duties better than anyone can even think of. We all know that at such a young age, where other girls are busy doing makeup, shopping and enjoying with their friends, you are busy working and earning money for your family. If you ask me, it's great! I wish I had children like you. At the same time, you should give a little more time to your course books too. We all will help you as much as we can, we'll give you good marks in the practicals, but the rest you'll have to take care of yourself.'

I replied nervously, 'I promise, ma'am. I'll take care of my studies.'

I thanked everybody in the room and left. On my way to my second canteen, Yamuna, I kept thinking about Sadhna ma'am's words from a few minutes ago.

I knew that she was right and I was glad that she was so thoughtful. When she had mentioned shopping and makeup, I remembered how I had forgotten those words. I couldn't even remember the last time I stood in front of a mirror to see how I looked. I hardly noticed my appearance anymore. My circumstances had made me mature before my age. I didn't know whether it was a bad or a good thing, but my circumstances had taught me how to struggle in this society and I still feel grateful for that.

I was so immersed in my thoughts that I didn't even realize when I reached Yamuna canteen. The auto driver's voice dragged me out of my reverie, although I think he called me a few times before I heard him and alighted from the auto. As I entered Yamuna canteen, I saw it was full of students. It looked like the general coach of a Mumbai local train. There was no space to sit, not even enough space to walk. Somehow, I managed to reach the kitchen of the canteen, where everyone was busy preparing samosas. I saw Roshni, heavily sweating and occupied with charging the students for their orders. I wondered how she was managing such a rush. I told one of the workers in the kitchen to handle the counter and called Roshni aside.

I took the canteen's feedback from her. She smiled and said, 'You can see for yourself how it's running.' Like Mohan Ji, she handed me the cash as well. When I counted it, I was amazed to find out that Yamuna had made Rs. 20,000 in just a month, which was quite remarkable. I handed Roshni everyone's salaries and left.

My entire day was spent visiting all my canteens. I felt super excited, yet super tired as well. I went to mom at the end of the day, took out all the cash from my purse and shouted in excitement, 'Mom, look at my canteens' collection from last month!'

When I handed Rs. 50,000 to mom, I could see tears forming in her eyes. Mom hugged me and said, 'I am so proud of you, Mehak.'

I was pleased that I had finally been able to bring a smile to my mom's face. She chuckled and said, 'You need to open an account. Don't keep this much cash at home.'

'First, I have to return the money that Saurav deposited at the time of your hospitalization. Then, I'll deposit the remaining amount in the bank.'

I called Saurav up and requested him to come home in the evening. I didn't want him to feel that I had called him just to return his money, so I thought of cooking something good for him. We hadn't enjoyed together in a really long time, so I decided to make a small party out of it.

I wanted to prepare a particular dish that I had learned, called 'Balti Paneer'. Despite my tiredness, thus, I went to the market with Sahil and Khushboo and bought the required vegetables, a family pack of ice cream, and a few sweets which Sahil and Khushboo loved. For the first time in my life, I bought a new music CD with the latest movie songs. While roaming in the market, Sahil saw a chocolate shop and started demanding some. He requested me for a single pack of chocolate, but I bought him two instead. He screamed with excitement, 'Yeee! Thank you, Didi.'

On reaching home, I started preparing for the party. A few minutes later, I heard our doorbell ring. I was in the kitchen, so I let mom open the door. I heard Sahil and Khushboo shouting and wondered what could be the reason. I came out of the kitchen to see everyone playing with a small puppy. I loved dogs and that puppy was just too cute. It was a white fur'd Pomeranian dog. I rushed towards it and saw Saurav standing there and smiling. I confusedly exchanged glances with him and mom. Mom said, 'Khushboo once told Saurav that she loves dogs, and see he gifted this puppy to her.'

I stared at Saurav. Here I was trying to pay him back his money, and there he continued doing things which kept me in his debt. Khushboo was very happy, so I didn't want to make her sad by returning the dog. In fact, I too had fallen in love with that puppy. I went to Saurav and asked, 'How much did you spend on purchasing this puppy?'

He retorted, 'Why do you always talk about money, Mehak? Do relations not matter to you?'

He looked very pissed, so I said, 'I didn't mean that. I just asked out of curiosity.'

He replied angrily, 'I have two dogs at home and a month back, Eve gave birth to nine puppies. Khushboo was once asking aunty for a dog, so I thought I'd bring her one.'

I thanked him for his thoughtfulness and invited him to dinner.

All of us had a blast eating food that night and enjoying ourselves while playing with our new puppy, Jimmy. (Yes, that is what I named him.) When Saurav was leaving, I returned him his Rs. 15,000 and thanked him for being so awesome.

He smiled and said, 'I still love you, Mehak. Give me a chance, please.'

I was puzzled and thought it to be the right time to tell him about Karthik. I told him everything that had happened at office after he left. Saurav listened to me dumbstruck. Even after I finished, he didn't react. He simply looked down without uttering a single word. His silence confused and bothered me, so I said, 'Saurav, say something please.' He looked up when I kept on requesting him. There were tears in his eyes. I didn't know what to do or say. I held his hand and said, 'You are my best friend, Saurav. I will always need your support and care, but please try to understand, I have no idea how to forget Karthik.'

He looked straight into my eyes and said, 'I don't want you to forget Karthik. It's just that I wish I could get a girl like you, one who would love me so much.'

'Saurav, I am sure you'll soon find a girl who'll love you more than anyone can,' I smiled.

Wiping his tears with a handkerchief, he chuckled, 'I too wish the same.'

The next day, mom and I went to a nearby bank and opened a savings account. I deposited the remaining amount in it and started a fully flowing business.

***

There is a saying that lousy time always seems to pass slowly, while good times pass by like a fraction of a second. I didn't realise how quickly two years passed after I opened Ganga, my first canteen. I became more mature regarding the operations of my business. My primary focus was on managing all my canteens properly. I was completely occupied with providing delicious food at economical prices. I started with snacks and introduced many new dishes over a period of time.

After two years of rigorous work, every canteen of mine started serving a full menu of main course dishes. I designed the menus depending upon the size of college and the number of students studying there. The bigger colleges with more than 1000 students were served the full menu which included 20 dishes, while the colleges which had less than 1000 students were served a simple menu which included only three types of thalis. Luckily, this strategy worked well and the figures in my savings account shot upwards by three lakh rupees. My family situation became a lot better too. For the first time on mom's birthday, I was able to gift her a new television and a refrigerator.

On Sundays, I would spend the whole day studying. On the rest of the days, I tried to study for at least an hour, but it was impossible most of the time. Before exams, I really had to study thoroughly to pass. I knew that my scores were very low, but I was happy that I was able to at least pass all the exams. My dreams had also evolved according to my circumstances. Now, all I could think of was to expand my business.

Sahil and Khushboo were busy studying too. Khushboo had turned out to be a very bright student. She scored 90% in her 10th board exams and opted for science and maths for further studies. Sahil was not that good in studies, but I was happy that he always tried to do well. I had a lot of expectations from Khushboo. She was among the brightest students at DAV school. As I had promised myself, I provided her with all the necessary support and resources like a good coaching, the right study environment and anything else which could help her achieve her targets. Mom had grown completely fit too. She came back to handle the mess with full force, like she had been doing it before. I didn't want to take any chances with her health again, so I hired two more guys to help her at the mess.

Everything was running smoothly. I couldn't remember the last time our lives had been like this. Saurav proved to be a great friend. Since I had told him about Karthik, he never mentioned that he loved me. He was entirely different from the other boys. He understood that Karthik was the only guy I could ever love. In the last two years, he had helped us like we were his family. He was always there when anyone of us needed him. We had bonded beautifully in a beneficial relationship called friendship.

Ganga was proving to be a hit, so my primary focus was to expanding its reach. In the food industry, that meant getting as much publicity as possible. So, I decided to open Ganga for the rest of the public too, but I could only do it with Sadhna ma'am's permission. She heard my concept with genuine interest and said, 'Mehak, I can't take this decision on my own. Opening Ganga within my college was under my authority, but opening it for the public requires the state government's permission.'

She advised me to write an application to the state office, mentioning all the details of Ganga. I wrote a complete application. I gave my form to her and she told me to wait for a response for about 15 days. This feeling of officialdom reminded me of my time at my old office.

I realized that it had been a long time since I had a chat with Nupur or Mohit sir. As soon as I came out of Sadhna ma'am's office, I dialled Nupur's number. She answered, 'Hi Mehak, so nice to hear your voice after so long. How are you now?'

'I am doing good, ma'am. How are things at your end?'

After a few other perfunctory questions and formal talk, I came to the point and said, 'Ma'am, I want to meet you. When can I come to the office?'

She laughed and said, 'Anytime you want, dear.'

I decided to go there right at that moment. I made my way to Nupur's cabin after a sweet conversation with Vaibhav and some of my old colleagues. I was delighted to see Nupur after such a long time. I told ma'am about the canteens I had opened at the different government colleges. I also told her about my canteen prizes and the items on the menu. Nupur was happy to see the growth I had made in this business. After telling her everything, I said, 'There is no canteen at our office either. Some employees bring food from home, while some eat at the restaurants nearby. Why don't we open a small mess here within the office.'

'That's a good idea. In fact, Mohit has been looking for someone who could open a small canteen in our office. What a coincidence! We have been looking all over Kota for the right person, when we should have come to our own Mehak,' Nupur sniggered.

The next day, I got a call from Nupur saying that everyone was on-board with setting up a canteen in the basement. She wanted me to start working on it right away.

When I told Saurav about opening a new canteen at our previous office, he laughed and replied teasingly, 'Is there any place in Kota that you'll leave? Or are you going to open a canteen in every society and by each road of the city?'

I angrily replied, 'Shut up, Saurav. Don't tease me.'

Unlike my other canteens, the prices in 'Jhelum' were on

the higher side. This was my first canteen at an office and unlike the students of government colleges, everybody earned money here. Yet, the prices were also higher. I hired three new workers and finally, mom inaugurated my fifth canteen.

At last, I had got my new assignment, something to keep my mind busy for a while. I thoroughly enjoyed my time at Jhelum. Being there felt like being with Karthik all over again. I recalled the days when I had been experiencing trauma and had lost all confidence in myself. Those were the days when Karthik brought me back to life from the depths of despair. As promised to Karthik, I always smiled whenever I missed him. Gradually, I started spending more time at 'Jhelum' than at the other canteens. It was as if I was hypnotized by his memories.

I spent almost ten continuous days at Jhelum. That began affecting the business at other canteens. This I realized when I got a call from the principal of Choti Maharani Girls School that a few students had been served stale samosas at Narmada. That was the first time that someone had complained about the food in my canteens. I was very pissed at what had happened. I reached Narmada, picked up a samosa and smelled it. She had been right, the potatoes used to make those samosas were indeed rotten. I shouted, 'Who the hell used these rotten potatoes?' No one said a single word. I was not a bad boss, so I continued politely, 'I have opened this canteen with a lot of hard work. Please don't do anything which can spoil my canteen's reputation.'

When everyone looked at my sad face, the workers said sorry and promised me not to repeat such an incident in future. I went to the principal and apologized for what had happened. After settling down everything, I was going home when I got a call from Sadhna ma'am. I hoped it to be regarding the permission for opening Ganga for everyone, so I quickly picked up her call in excitement. I said cheerfully, 'Hello, ma'am. Good evening.'

'Hi, Mehak. Can you come and meet me tomorrow?' I felt a certain seriousness in her tone.

I replied, 'I can come right now if you'd like.'

'It's not that urgent,' she said, 'You can come tomorrow morning.'

***

'Mehak, I got a reply to the application we had sent to the state government's office,' Sadhna Ma'am told me while I was sitting in her office the next morning.

I curiously replied, 'What was the reply, ma'am?'

'They said that they were not aware of any canteen running at Government Girl's College, so there was no question of opening it for everyone. Secondly, if there indeed is any such canteen that is making money from a government institution, it'll have to pay a monthly rent to the government according to the rule. They want you to deposit a rent from the day you opened Ganga, then only they'll see to what lies next.'

'That's not possible, ma'am,' I replied, astounded.

Wiping sweat from her face, she said, 'To permit you to start the canteen was within my power; I don't know how they can do this. There must be something wrong, I need to figure it out. You don't worry, we'll find a way out.'

I didn't understand what had gone wrong or what mistake I had made. One day, I was at Ganga when ma'am came to me and said, 'You know, Mehak, why those guys sent us that kind of a reply?'

I had no idea, so I asked, 'Why?'

'That idiot, Mr. Sharma from Law College, complained about your canteen. Those guys at the state government's office had been waiting for the right time. When we sent them that letter, they got their chance and sent us that kind of a reply. But the thing I don't understand is why Mr. Sharma complained about Ganga.'

I then told her about the incident with Mr. Sharma where he had asked me for a bribe. She was shocked to hear it. She nodded her head and said, 'Now I see why he is so pissed with you. You are among the fewest to have denied him a bribe. Mr. Sharma might have someone in the department who works for him and is responsible for that letter.'

'What should I do now?' I asked.

She considered it for a few seconds and then replied, 'Mehak, you are in business now. You'll need to be a little cunning and strong. When you climb the ladder of success, you will come across many who'd be jealous of you and would want to destroy your happiness at any cost. You have to learn how to tackle such people. My suggestion would be that you call him and tell him to stop bothering you like this. Tell him that you will inform the police about the matter otherwise.'

I wanted to follow her advice, but I did not feel strong enough to stand up to a powerful man like that. I felt worried that he might have such connections that if I threatened him, he might do something even worse to me. On the other hand, however, if I didn't do anything, I would have to pay a lot of money to the government. I had been running my business honestly and without cheating anybody, then why should I have to spend so much money, I thought.

Mr. Sharma was a corrupt man who wanted a bribe. I didn't know what to do, so I said, 'Ma'am, you are right. I have to raise my voice against such an unethical thing. But what if he takes another way to destroy my business?'

'I am with you, Mehak, but you'll have to take the initiative. Otherwise, they will all blame me that you would have given a bribe but for my support.'

'I'll have to do something, ma'am, and I have decided that I will stand up against this unethical thing.'

After discussing the issue with mom and getting a thumbs up from her, I dialled Mr. Sharma's number. No one answered the first time. I tried again. The second time, a guy picked up the phone and said, 'Hello, Mr. Sharma's office.'

I confidently replied, 'I wish to speak with Mr. Sharma.'

'Hello, Sharma here.'

I stammered, 'Mr. Sharma, I am Mehak.'

He paused for a second and said, 'Mehak, why have you called me?'

'Mr. Sharma, why are you maligning my reputation and trying to extort money from me by illegal means?'

'Listen, Mehak. You must be mistaken. I am not that kind of a person. Why would I do such a terrible thing?' he laughed.

'Whatever! Mr. Sharma, let me tell you one thing very clearly. If you think that you can get away with anything just because I am a girl, then you are wrong. I can complain to the police that you were forcing me to bribe you and when I said no, you threatened me. Just imagine what would happen to you if I did such a thing,' I said, having gathered all my courage.

'Are you trying to threaten me, Mehak?' I could feel the seriousness in his voice.

'No, Mr. Sharma. I am just trying to say that you shouldn't get in the way of other people's dreams, especially when they are working so hard to fulfil them. Please let me work in peace, have the fear of God. Otherwise, I will have to do something which I don't want to do,' I replied as fast as I could and hung up.

***

A few days later, Sadhna ma'am informed me that I had got the permission to open Ganga for everyone. As per the law, however, I had to pay Rs. 3000 as rent.

I called up my mom and Saurav to tell them the good news. I couldn't contain my excitement upon reaching home and flitted about excitedly. We needed to do a little marketing for Ganga, so everybody would come to know that it was now open to the general public. I ordered 20 posters and banners as part of our little marketing initiative. I got the posters in three days. Looking at one of the posters I had ordered, I couldn't help but smile.

'Ganga—a symbol of pureness'

'Experience the taste of delicious food with Ganga like purity at our Ganga canteen.'

We placed these posters and banners at all the nearby places. Our present location was not big enough, so I took a bigger place near the college to run all operations from.

I hired a few more workers and bought new tables and chairs. For the first few days, our customers were mostly students. We hardly noticed any customers from outside. A month passed and we didn't get the kind of response we had been expecting, but as they say—one has to maintain their patience in business. One can't hope to get positive feedback right from the very beginning.

My patience gradually paid off. Every year, our college organized a fest to which all the students and their parents were invited. Every year, it experienced a footfall of about 5000 visitors who came to the college to attend the fest. During the fest, all the people that came to the college got a chance to taste Ganga's food. And as per their feedback, they really liked it.

Just after the fest, we noticed a lot of outside customers coming in and their number started increasing day by day.

I started cooking food at Ganga myself as I didn't want to take any chances which could ruin my reputation. We noticed a 70% increase in profits, which meant that I started earning about Rs. 1 Lakh every month from Ganga itself.

One day, I was not feeling well, so I decided to take a day's leave from work and rest at home. I was lying on my bed thinking about my work, of what to do next and how to do something different. Suddenly, I got a call from Saurav. I quickly picked up the call and said, 'You idiot! Where have you been? It's been 15 days since we met last.'

'I am here only, yaar. Just occupied with a lot of official travel,' he laughed.

'So busy that you don't have any time for friends, evil Saurav.'

'I have something important to tell you, Mehak. When can we meet?' he asked.

'I am at home. Come over,' I quickly said.

'No, not at home. Somewhere outside…' he chuckled.

'Okay, fine. Come to Ganga then. You forgot we have our own restaurant now,' I laughed.

I wanted to rest, but since it was Saurav and I hadn't met him for such a long time, I decided to go. I quickly got ready and took an auto to Ganga. As always, Saurav was there already. I smiled and said, 'Before time, as always.'

'For you, it's always before time. Madam, you own six canteens now. Buy a car, please?' he sniggered.

'Why do I need a car? Whenever I have to go somewhere by car, I'll call you,' I winked.

'I am always at your service, Mehak Ji. Accha, do you know why I wanted to meet you today?'

I hastily replied, 'No, stupid. Tell me quickly.'

'I wanted to introduce you to someone.'

I had been talking to Saurav for the last five minutes without noticing anyone standing there besides us. When he stretched his hand, I finally noticed the girl standing next to him.

She held Saurav's hand and walked closer to us. I looked at both of them in confusion. Saurav smiled and said, 'Meet Moksha, my girlfriend.'

As a reflex, a 'what' came out of my mouth. I came to my senses soon enough and replied, 'Hi Moksha, you are so beautiful.'

We chatted for the next half an hour. I ordered food for everyone. After eating Ganga's special paneer tikka, Moksha said, 'This is the tastiest paneer tikka I have ever had. Is this restaurant new?'

Saurav winked at me and said, 'She doesn't know anything.'

Saurav then turned to Moksha and said, 'This is Mehak's restaurant and she is an excellent cook.'

'What? I thought you are a college student,' Moksha replied in an astonished manner.

I smiled and replied, 'Do you see that building next to the restaurant? I study at that college.'

Saurav and Moksha told me that they had been dating for the last six months. They had first met at a wedding ceremony where their families introduced them to each other. Both their families knew about their relationship and they were to get married soon. When they left, I sat down quietly thinking about them and how lucky they were to have found each other. I was happy that Saurav had finally moved on and had found someone who loved him very much. Suddenly, I started missing Karthik, and a few tears fell from my eyes.

***

Over the next three months, my target was to take Ganga to new heights and I kept myself fully immersed in that project.

It was like any other evening and I was sitting at Ganga. I usually went home by 9 o'clock. I loved making dinner with my family. That day, I was about to leave for home when I heard a few voices coming from the sitting area of the restaurant. I came out of the kitchen and saw a few girls shouting at Mohan Ji. I quickly went over to them and asked Mohan Ji, 'What happened?'

One of the girls shouted, 'This idiot is arguing with us.'

I looked confusedly at Mohan Ji. He said, 'They are drinking in here.'

I had always wanted my canteens to be pure and alcohol-free, so I requested them politely, 'Ma'am, alcohol consumption is not allowed here. I request you to please booze outside the premises, and then you can come in here to eat.'

Another one of the girls rudely replied, 'Look, waiter, we don't want to argue with you. Just get lost.'

I graciously replied again, 'Ma'am, I am the owner of this restaurant. Please step outside before I summon the watchman.'

Suddenly, they all started laughing and said, 'Oh, owner? Look at you, behen ji. We didn't know this canteen was owned by a behen ji. Otherwise, we would never have come here.'

Still laughing at me, they all left. I turned to Mohan Ji and said, 'I am sorry, Mohan Ji, about their behaviour.'

I didn't wait for Mohan Ji to reply and left myself. The sound of their laughter kept ringing in my ears all the way back home. Upon reaching, I quietly went to my room and looked at myself in the mirror. I was wearing a white Salwar Kurta and had hardly any sign of makeup on me.

That whole night, their words kept piercing at my heart. Somehow, their words had changed my perspective. I decided to change myself, so that one would think a hundred times before calling me behen ji in future.

My target was to earn more and more money now. I understood that if you wanted to earn respect, power, and status, you had to earn a lot of money. I also realized that people will always judge you by the way you look and live, and not by the kind of person you are. I had been living a very simple life until then. I dressed simply, I lived simply, and my life-style was completely devoid of showing-off, which is why a few drunk girls could gather the audacity to call me behen ji. My desires had changed now. I wanted to buy a new car, I wanted to look good. I had accepted that to survive in this world, you had to be a show-off, only then would people start taking you seriously.

The New Me

I spent the whole of the next day shopping. I had bought so many clothes for myself for the first time in my life. My plan was to change my entire wardrobe. After that, I went to the parlour and spent the rest of the day transforming myself.

When I reached home and ringed the doorbell, Sahil opened the door while playing on his video game. He took one quick look at me and shouted, 'Mom, some girl is at the door,' and left. Mom had been in the kitchen. When she came out and looked at me, she shouted, 'Mehak, what happened to you?'

'How do I look, mom?' I asked her.

'You look so dashing, just like a movie actress,' mom laughed.

When Khushboo saw me, she screamed, 'Di, you look beautiful.'

I got the same reaction from everyone else. When I went to Ganga, Mohan Ji looked at me, smiled and said, 'Ma'am, you are looking good, but you don't have to change yourself completely just because those girls said something. That

Mehak has a lot of potential, don't let her get lost in all this.'

With a new look, I had stretched my goals and dimensions. Ganga was very popular now. It had started as a small canteen, but had now turned into a big one that served approximately 200 customers daily with a total monthly profit of Rs. 3 to 4 Lakhs. All the canteens together started accumulating a monthly sum of Rs. 7 to 8 Lakhs. At Ganga, we started a feedback system. After every meal, we requested the customer to fill out a feedback form and write their comments. We then evaluated those forms on a monthly basis. Many customers asked us to make it a more family friendly place.

The canteen model had its own limitations though. I wasn't able to change it into a full-fledged family restaurant. So, I finally took the most important decision of my life. I decided that I wanted to open a restaurant now. I had already accumulated enough money to do it, so I didn't have to worry about the finances.

I started looking for a suitable site for the restaurant. I knew that buying land and then building a restaurant on it was not a good idea. I was more interested in a place where I could start the operations after only a little renovation. Property dealers suggested many places, but I didn't like them much when I visited them. Wherever I went, I was always on the lookout for potential places.

***

One day, while coming home after finishing work, my eyes caught sight of a building on the right side of the flyover. I instructed the auto driver to stop. It was a place on the 4th floor of a building. It was ideal for rooftop dining. I loved it at the first look itself. I asked the watchmen there, 'Bhaiya, who is the owner of this building?'

He replied, 'Saxena sahib,' while spitting tobacco on the road.

'Is he here right now?'

'No, he lives in Delhi.'

'I want his number.'

'Go to the 1st floor,' he quickly replied.

I went to a small cabin on the first floor. A lady was sitting there. I knocked on the door and heard a sweet voice, 'Come in.'

As I entered, I saw a girl who was hardly my age. She looked at me and said, 'Yes, how can I help you?'

'I was wondering if you can give me the contact details of Mr. Saxena.'

She politely replied, 'Sure, you can note down his number.'

'May I also please see the rooftop of this building?' I asked her.

'Yes, sure. Come, I'll show you,' she smiled.

The view from the top was excellent. I closed my eyes and imagined that place with a lot of people eating food, with soothing music playing in the background. I decided to get this place for my new restaurant.

I thanked her and left. As soon as I reached home, I dialled Mr. Saxena's number. Someone picked up the call and said, 'Hello?'

'Am I speaking with Mr. Saxena?'

'Yes.'

'Mr. Saxena, my name is Mehak. I am calling from Kota. I saw your building near Bhawani circle today. I am looking for a place to rent for my new restaurant and I was wondering if you would be interested in something like that.'

Mr. Saxena cleared his throat and said, 'Mehak, I am more interested in giving that place out to coaching classes, not for a restaurant. People drink at restaurants and create a mess. I don't like all that.'

'My restaurant will be pure vegetarian and alcohol will be strictly prohibited,' I corrected him quickly.

'That's good, but I have already decided that I'll give it to some coaching institute.'

I liked that place very much and I didn't want to let it go, so I requested, 'Mr. Saxena, I like that place very much. Believe me, I'll take care of everything like you want me to. You don't have to worry at all.' He paused for a few seconds and then replied, 'I am coming to Kota next week to finalize this. Let's discuss it then itself.'

'Thank you, Mr. Saxena. I'll call you next week to fix up a meeting time.'

Then, I got hold of mom and told her to come with me.

Mom confusedly asked, 'Where are we going, Mehak?'

'It's a suspense. Now don't ask any questions, just wait and watch,' I chuckled.

Meanwhile, I texted Saurav and told him to come where we were going too. Mom was curious and asked the same question, 'Where are we going?' at least five times.

At last, we reached our destination. mom looked at me amazed and said, 'Car showroom?'

I smiled and said, 'Yes, Maa. You have struggled enough. From now on, you shall commute in a car.'

Mom looked at me astonished and replied, 'Are you serious, Mehak? Why spend so much money when we can travel by auto.'

'What is the use of earning money, maa, if it can't help in making your life easier?' I said in a convincing voice.

A few minutes later, Saurav reached there too. I saw a box in his hands and asked, 'What's in that?'

'Sweets, what else?' he winked.

I couldn't control my laughter and said, 'Couldn't you wait? What's the hurry?'

As we went in, a salesman came to us and said, 'Hello, Mehak ma'am. Hello ma'am, hello sir,' to me, mom and Saurav respectively.

Mom and Saurav stared at me. I smiled and said, 'I have already completed all the formalities, we just have to take the car home today.'

Mom was shocked and asked, 'How, Mehak, when, why?'

I hugged mom and replied, 'All this has only become possible because of your love and hard work. I wish everybody gets a mother like you.'

We were busy talking when that salesman returned and handed the car keys to mom. He smiled and said, 'Congratulations for the new car, ma'am,' and left. I could feel mom's happiness. After a long time, I was seeing her that happy. I too was happy from inside that I had done something which brought a smile to mom's face.

***

The day was Monday, and as discussed with Mr. Saxena, I called him. He told me to come to the same building at 11 o'clock.

I reached the building and went upstairs. I knocked the door of the same cabin and asked for Mr. Saxena. The girl ushered me towards a door to her right and said, 'He is coming, you can wait inside.'

I was waiting inside when suddenly, I heard the voice of someone opening the door. I thought it would be Mr. Saxena and stood up to greet him. When I looked at him, I couldn't stop my eyes from opening wide. He looked at me the same way. He was the first one to utter, 'What are you doing here?'

My question was more appropriate. 'Are you Mr. Saxena?'

'Yes.' Then he smiled and said, 'Small world.'

I smiled back at him and replied, 'Yes. I didn't expect you to see you here, uncle.'

***

I quickly went to mom, hugged her and said, 'We got that place for our new restaurant.'

'Wow! Congratulations, Mehak,' Mom replied.

She then continued, 'But when you had called him last week, he told you that he wanted to give that place to a coaching institute.'

'Yes. You won't believe what happened,' I started laughing. When I couldn't control my laughter, mom finally asked in exasperation, 'Mehak, tell me what happened.'

Somehow, I composed myself and replied, 'Do you remember when I went to Delhi a few years ago for my colleague Vaibhav's wedding?

'Yes.'

'Mr. Saxena is the uncle of Vaibhav's wife, Meera. During one of the functions, Mr. Saxena's wife lost her diamond necklace somewhere. She was really upset and crying while looking for it everywhere. Saxena uncle was worried too because it was worth Rs. 1 Lakh. After the function, I was sitting in the lawn with my colleagues. I was feeling thirsty, so I went to the water cooler near the same hall where the function had happened the same morning. When I was coming back, my foot struck something under the carpet. I found it to be her lost necklace! I then went to them and returned it. Everyone thanked me profusely for that, especially uncle and aunty.'

Mom smiled upon hearing that incident. She took a sigh of relief and said, 'So there was no way that Mr. Saxena could say no to you.'

'Yes!' I shouted. I was amazed at how destiny could solve all my significant problems in just a few minutes. Getting the place I desired was the best example of this. Saxena uncle was so happy to see me that he instantly offered the place to me, and at a lower rent as well.

Now, it was time for me to face my next challenge. I wanted to establish my new restaurant as the best place to eat in Kota, but for that, I had to do everything correctly.

I called Saurav and told him about the new place I had just rented. I also asked him if he could come home for a few discussions. He was at work then and said that he would come in the evening.

We had to do all the planning and made a list of all the things we needed to do. I was sitting quietly, immersed in my thoughts, when mom said, 'Mehak, you are expanding your business and I can't help you that much. I think you need a helping hand. Why don't you ask Saurav to join you in this business?'

A few minutes later, I found myself thinking about the same thing. I replied, 'Yes, you are right. Let's talk to him when he comes.'

Mom and I got so busy in this discussion that we didn't realize when the afternoon changed into evening. When Saurav arrived, I showed him the picture of the place I had rented. He smiled and said, 'This place looks so nice, yaar. Where have you found a place like this in Kota?'

I told him the whole incident and my encounter with Saxena uncle. I felt a little hesitant to ask Saurav about the partnership, as I didn't want to bring money matters between our friendship. At the same time, I needed someone to help me with the business. I asked hesitatingly, 'As you know, Saurav, the business is growing and I need somebody to help me with it. You are the only one who comes to my mind when I think of a partner.'

He stared at me and asked, 'Are you serious, Mehak?'

'I am very serious, Mom thinks so too,' I replied, looking at mom.

Mom nodded her head. I continued, 'We will share our profits.'

Saurav smiled and said, 'You are very innocent, Mehak. When I am not investing any money in your restaurant, how can I share the profits?'

I looked at him and said, 'How do you want to do it then, you tell me?'

'Our friendship is above money. Whenever you need any help, I'll always be there. Don't think that you are alone in this project. I promise you, I'll take full responsibility for whatever work you assign me,' he replied smiling.

'I know, Saurav, you are always there, but it doesn't look good if you help me out so much and not take any money in return.'

He chuckled and replied, 'Never compare relationships with money. Here is the deal, you can give me an exact amount every month on the 30th.'

We all laughed at his sense of humour. I replied, 'Done, but one day, I want you to enter into a serious partnership with me.'

'Let's keep it as my promise, Mehak. We will work together one day, the day I have money to invest. Now, let's list down the priority tasks quickly.'

Our location was a rooftop, so we needed to create a complimentary ambience. We decided to hire a designer who could take care of the ambience, which also included the colour of tables and chairs.

Saurav said, 'If you want, we can hire the designer who designed our restaurant Eatos?'

'Eatos' interior is nice. Let's call him today itself,' I quickly replied.

'What about the name and the head chef?' Mom asked.

I knew that mom and I couldn't cook there every day. We required a good chef and a few cooks to assist him. Saurav sniggered and said, 'In the food industry, you need to steal chefs and cooks. My dad always does this. Whenever he requires new cooks, he goes to all the restaurants and wherever he likes the food, he hires that cook and doubles his salary.''

'But that's cheating,' I said.

'Yeah, but that is how things work in this industry,' he replied, shaking his head.

'Let's do it that way then. It will take time though. In the meantime, let's finalize the name?'

Everyone had different opinions. Mom suggested a name, I wanted something else, while Saurav liked something unique.

After a lot of debate on various names and their meanings, we went into mythologies, histories, and travelled the whole universe with our ideas. After about half an hour, I realized that we had diverted from our purpose. I stopped mom and Saurav in between and said, 'Please stop exploring mythologies, this is not a history class. I have finalized the name.'

They both said 'what' at the same time. I looked at both of them and said, 'Sampoorn.'

Saurav looked at me and said, 'Wow. Mehak. You are a genius. It's such a nice name.'

That night, I slept happy and satisfied. I was thrilled and excited about the opening of my new restaurant.

Sampoorn

The idea of stealing a cook from a good restaurant sounded a little weird to me, but that was the only feasible option I could see. I didn't know where to start, so I called Saurav and we made a list of 15 good restaurants that we knew in Kota. We had to complete a lot of work over the next three months, so I was a little tensed about managing things.

Kota ranges from 'Rangbadi' to 'Station' and from 'Vigyan Nagar' to 'Thermal power plant', so we decided to start from Rangbadi. We first went to 'Tadka', a restaurant with excellent interiors. We ordered very basic dishes to judge the taste, but unfortunately, we were disappointed. The food there was remarkably regular, which anyone could prepare at home.

One by one, we visited seven restaurants. After visiting every restaurant, we checked out its name from the list that we had prepared. After eating a little bit at so many restaurants, our stomachs were so full that I would have puked if somebody had made me eat another morsel of food. We decided to cover the rest of the restaurants the next day.

The time was 6 o'clock already. It had taken us six hours to cover seven restaurants and it was damn tiring. We had to take the designer to our location too for site inspection. He carefully inspected every corner of the rooftop and said, 'I can make this place look like you are sitting at a restaurant in Miami.'

I was happy to hear that and replied, 'That's cool. But my only concern is that Kota gets very hot during the summers. How can we keep this place cool?'

'You don't worry about that. We can install air coolers which are specially manufactured for these kind of restaurants,' he casually replied.

'Come on Mehak, wake up! We have to eat a lot of food today.' Saurav called me up at 8 o'clock in the morning and shouted through the phone.

I looked at my watch and replied, 'It is 8 o'clock. Not a single restaurant is open at this time.'

He laughed and replied, 'I am extra excited. As you know, I love eating. Anyway, you get ready. I'll be there by 11 o'clock, okay?'

We visited a few restaurants again. I looked at my watch, got irritated and asked Saurav, 'Yaar, we have visited six restaurants and everywhere, the chef sucks. What are we going to do and where will we find our guy?'

'Have patience, my dear. Where there is a will, there's a way. Let's go for a drive. Look, it's raining,' Saurav tried to convince me.

I opened the window of the car and felt drops of water on my hand. The smell of fresh rain on dry ground filled my nostrils. I took a deep breath, inhaling as much fresh air as I could. I heard the sounds of thunder and saw the tress dancing in the rain. It looked like they were celebrating the monsoon too. I badly wanted to get drenched in the rain, so I shouted, 'Hey, let's go out and enjoy the rain.'

Saurav smiled and replied, 'Are you serious?'

I held his hand and pulled him out of the car. The rain was torrential, and within five minutes, we were soaking wet. I was singing and dancing in the rain. In all that excitement, I forgot that I was on the road. I saw a few roadside kids looking at me and smiling. I waved at them and sat inside the car. We were all wet and craved for a hot cup of tea, so I said, 'Hey, let's go for a cup of tea.'

We had started from the middle of Kota, but soon crossed the last reaches of it. We were on the national highway to Jaipur. I was still drenched and badly needed a hot cup of tea, so I again said, 'it's cold here and I want a cup of tea. Please stop somewhere.'

Saurav thought about something for two minutes and replied, 'have you heard about Shekhawati Dhaba near Badgaon?'

'I have heard of Badgaon, but I have never heard of Shekhawati. What's that?'

Saurav was surprised, and replied, 'It's a very famous dhaba. When I was in college, we used to go there with friends a lot. You'll love the food there.'

After such appreciation, I could not say no to it. 'If it is that good, let's go and see.'

It was still raining heavily, and there was water everywhere. After about a fifteen minute drive through puddles and potholes, we reached Shekhawati. It was not much, a small hut and a small open kitchen to the right of it, where men were busy preparing food. The cooks were in a red turban, which indicated that they all belonged to old Rajasthani tribes. I saw a few truck drivers sitting on the traditional 'Khat' and eating their food. The seating arrangement there was quite traditional too. We went in and sat on a Khat too.

We ordered a traditional dish, as suggested by Saurav. A few minutes later, a guy arrived with two large plates and kept them in front of us. They were triple the size of the normal plates that we used at homes. The whole plate was full of different items; daal, two types of chutney, a gravy dish and their traditional raita or butter milk. One plate of their food was enough for three people, so I asked, 'How can anyone eat this whole Thali?'

He smiled and replied, 'Don't worry, I'll help you.'

When I took a small piece of baati, dipped it in daal and ate it, a 'wow' escaped my mouth. I couldn't believe that the daal could be that tasty. I knew how to prepare excellent daal, but this was something else entirely. One by one, I tasted all the things, and everything had a unique taste which is very rare to find these days. In this modern world, the definition of food and the ways to prepare ethnic dishes has changed. New cooks have come up and introduced new recipes and ideas to make food.

Before I tasted all those dishes, I had thought that I was a good cook, but now I was forced to believe that food can be made even more delicious. I knew that I had got my new chef. I went to the cashier and asked him, 'Bhaiya, who cooked this food?'

He looked at me in confusion and replied with an accent, 'Madam ji, is there a problem with the food?'

I didn't know how to speak his dialect, but having been born and brought up in Rajasthan, I could easily understand it. I smiled and replied, 'No bhaiya, the food was great. I just want to meet the cook.'

He relaxed on hearing that and shouted, 'Bhola, a customer liked your food and wants to meet you. Come outside!'

I went back to my seat. Saurav looked at me curiously, trying to guess what I was doing. He said, 'Mehak, please don't tell me that you are trying to hire a cook from this dhaba.'

I winked and replied, 'Your guess is right. I am thinking of doing exactly that.'

'Come on, Mehak! You are opening a niche rooftop restaurant. How can a guy who doesn't even understand Hindi handle customers who'll speak in English? And this would also ruin the reputation of your restaurant when people see you chef to be some villager,' Saurav said.

I was about to reply when I saw an old man coming towards us. He was wearing a white dhoti and kurta, along with the traditional Rajasthani turban. He looked like he was in his 60's. Old enough to be our grandfather, I thought. He walked up to me and said, 'Namaste, madam ji.'

I felt nice seeing him. I had never seen my grandfather, but imagined that he must look something like him. I chuckled and said, 'Bhola Ji, you cook delicious food. You have been blessed with the art of cooking.'

He smiled and said, 'Thank you for liking the food. I don't know if I have an art or not, but I am uneducated and cooking was the only thing I knew, so I started doing it.'

He seemed to be an honest man. I asked, 'What else can you cook?'

'All Rajasthani dishes.'

I wanted to know how much he earned there, so I asked him bluntly, 'How much do you earn here?'

He seemed confused, but replied, '4000 Rupees and free meals.'

'Where is your family?'

'I live with two of my kids at a nearby village.'

'Where is your wife?'

'She is no more,' he replied, looking at the sky.

'Do you want to earn more?'

'Madam Ji, who in this world doesn't want to earn more? Yes, I have kids to feed.'

'Would you like to work at my restaurant? I'll give you Rs. 10,000 a month with free meals too.'

He paused for a few seconds and replied, 'The owner of this restaurant gave me a job when I had nowhere else to go. How can I leave him? Money is not everything for me, madam ji.'

I was impressed with his loyalty. I had been looking for exactly that sort of a person. I quickly replied, 'That's true, but as you just said, everyone wants to earn more money. You can send your kids to school and earn well if you work with me.'

'I know, but I can't leave him on such short notice. I need a month's time to repay his kindness.'

I was confused about what he meant by that, so I asked, 'And how will you do that?'

'I'll work for free for this one month,' he smiled.

I noticed Saurav's eyes getting wide when he heard that. I smiled and said, 'Bhola Ji, can you work for me after that?'

'Yes, why not?'

I smiled and took out Rs. 2000 as token money. I stretched my hand to him and said, 'Here's some money for you as the advance.'

He tried to refuse it, but I gave him the money forcefully and left. On our way back, I looked at Saurav. He seemed pissed off with my decision to hire a village guy as our chef. I asked him, 'Why are you so upset, yaar?'

He stared at me and replied, 'How can you take such a big risk and that too for your dream restaurant?'

I chuckled, 'How can you say that, yaar? A cook is a cook. How is an educated cook different from a cook who is uneducated and belongs to a village?'

'It does not affect me, but it affects a lot of people. When they see that a chef is from a village, they raise questions about the hygiene of the restaurant.'

'That's all rubbish. Just because of this biased society, the talented villagers aren't able to improve their conditions by earning a better income. I don't want to support all these biases. I will give every deserving person a fair chance.'

Saurav didn't say anything. I continued, 'Saurav, I know that you are my best friend and want everything to go smoothly, but you'll have to trust me on this. Do you trust me?'

He smiled and said, 'I trust you, baba. Let's give him a chance.'

***

Opening a restaurant requires a lot of permissions from the government, and my previous experiences with the government had involved a lot of time and of course, a lot of bribes too. I requested Saurav to ask his father about the permissions that we had to take.

Saurav gave me a paper which said, 'Obtaining approvals'. He had noted down the permissions that we were required to take. I carefully read the paper.

1. Local Police Department: Demonstrating to them that you have the permission from the landowner to start a restaurant.

2. Plan to Municipal Corporation: Submit a plan of your restaurant. Municipal Corporation then gives you the utilization certificate, and the trade & health license.

3. Permission from the Fire Department: Stating that they don't have any objection to your operating as a restaurant at the location of your choice.

4. Participate in Shop Act Programme: To ensure the workers' safety.

5. Food Standards and Safety Act: To obtain the certificates stating that all the people working at the restaurant are healthy. The government will do that examination every six months.

I felt nervous reading through all the permissions that I needed to take. I asked Saurav, 'How are we going to get all these permissions?'

Saurav confidently replied, 'Let's start with the police department first. I am sure we'll get all the permissions on time, you don't worry.'

The next morning, we went to the police station with the rental agreement. As we entered, we saw a man being beaten and abused badly. That man was crying and sobbing. I got scared and went out. Saurav came outside and asked, 'What happened?'

'I can't see these kind of things.'

'It's a police station, Mehak. What else did you expect to find here, a bhajan?'

We went in again. That policeman was now done with the beating, and was sitting on his desk. Saurav greeted him and said, 'Sir, how are you?'

He replied uncouthly, 'What do you want?'

Saurav stammered, 'We are opening a restaurant. Here is the rent agreement.'

He stared at me and replied, 'Is she your wife?'

He was continuously staring at me. I wanted to tell him to stop doing that, but we were there to get permission, so I stood silent.

Saurav assertively said, 'No sir, she is my friend. So I was saying, this is the agreement. We just wanted your permission.'

He blatantly laughed and replied, 'What will I do with this agreement, eat it?'

We both looked at each other in confusion. The cop continued, 'Do you know the rates for these kind of approvals? No? I'll tell you. 10,000 Rupees is the price. Send the money and take the approval. Now go, I have other things to do.'

I couldn't resist anymore and said, 'Why the 10,000, sir? We are not doing anything unethical or unlawful.'

He stared at me and replied, 'Ethical or unethical, we decide, madam. Now, get out of here.'

We came out of the police station, frustrated. As soon as we sat in the car, I shouted, 'What will we do now? I don't want to waste my money on these kind of people.'

Saurav was deep in thought. After a few minutes passed, he said, 'Let's go to my father. Maybe, he can help us.'

I knew that Saurav's father owned five restaurants in Kota and he was a well-known name in the restaurant industry, so I quickly said, 'Okay.'

For the first time, I went to Saurav's house. As I stopped the car, I saw a big white bungalow in front of me. It looked like the house they showed in movies where film stars lived.

Saurav, on the other hand, always lived very meagrely. I never saw him spending unnecessary money on anything, despite the fact that he easily could. I looked at Saurav and said, 'You know what I like the most in you?'

He was surprised at my weird question and asked, 'What?'

'You are so rich, but still you live so simply, earn your own money and then spend it.'

He smiled and replied, 'There's nothing like that.'

We entered into a big office where Saurav's dad was sitting and giving instructions to somebody. I didn't want to hear what he was saying, but he was talking too loudly to ignore. He was shouting at somebody, 'How can that bastard steal our chef, and you idiots let him go. I want him back. Go and burn his restaurant if you have to, but bring back my chef,' and he slammed the phone on his desk.

He looked at Saurav and said, 'What a pleasant surprise, beta. What are you doing here? Don't tell me you have finally decided to join my business.'

Saurav smiled and replied, 'Not again, papa.'

His dad looked at me and asked, 'Who is this beautiful girl with you?'

I greeted him, and Saurav said, 'She is Mehak.'

His dad looked at me and exclaimed in excitement, 'Oh! I've heard a lot about you, Mehak. How's your canteen? Let me know if you need any help.'

Saurav jumped into the discussion and said, 'Dad, she actually needs your help right now,' and told him the whole scene.

His dad listened to the whole thing. His face became a little serious. He looked at me and asked, 'Where are you opening your restaurant?'

'It's a rooftop location near Chawani Circle. The building is next to the Grand Chandiram Hotel.'

He raised his eyebrows in confusion and asked, 'Is that Saxena's building?'

I was shocked. I asked, 'Yes, but how did you know that?'

I could sense the anger in his eyes. He retorted, 'I have been trying to take that space for a restaurant for the last two months. He refused me every time, saying that he wanted to lend that space out to some coaching institute. How come he gave that space to you?'

I could hear the frustration in his voice that he didn't get what he wanted, but I got it instead. Saurav also detected the same and jumped into the conversation. He smiled and said, 'Paa, when Mehak first called Mr. Saxena, he said no to her too. She requested a lot, but he didn't agree. When they finally met, he turned out to be the uncle of Mehak's close friend, Vaibhav,' and so he narrated the whole story to his dad.

His dad thought about something for few seconds, laughed and then replied, 'That's great, you are a lucky girl. Don't worry, you leave everything to me. I'll get you all the permissions.'

I thanked him profusely and said, 'Uncle, I'll be highly obliged. Let me know if I can ever do anything for you.'

***

The interiors for Sampoorn were almost finished. Both Mom and Saurav liked the interiors. One day, we were discussing the pending tasks which needed to be completed as soon as possible. Everyone was thinking about what remained, when suddenly, Saurav shouted, 'We have to invite some VIP for the inauguration!'

Mom agreed and said, 'Yes, he is right. With this, we will be able to attract some attention too.'

Saurav then said, 'My dad knows a few MLAs and political giants. I can talk to him, if you want.'

I looked at both of them and replied, 'When I decided to open this restaurant, I also decided whom I wanted to invite for the inauguration.'

Both of them looked at me and asked, 'Who?'

'Karthik's grandfather.'

Saurav gave me a confused look, scratched his head and asked, 'Why his grandfather?'

'Because that's what Karthik wants.'

No one said a single word after that. Saurav was still thinking about what else remained to do and said, 'We need to give ads in the newspapers. We can also get some leaflets printed and distribute them to as many guys as we can.'

We decided the matter of the leaflets quickly. Saurav also suggested that we do aggressive marketing for the restaurant, to make it famous. We agreed on giving the leaflets to two of the top newspapers in Kota.

I was a little apprehensive, as only a week was left before the inauguration and the menu was yet to be fixed. I then remembered that Bhola Ji would arrive the next day. I was sure that he could help me set up an excellent menu.

The next day, as expected, he called me up and asked me the address of Sampoorn. An hour later, he was in front of me. He carefully looked around the whole restaurant and said in his typical hadoti accent, 'Madam Ji, this place is looking very nice.'

I smiled and replied, 'Thanks, but we'll have to serve the customers delicious food to run it well.'

He confidently said, 'Don't worry, I'll take care of that.'

***

For the next two days, we carefully decided the menu, keeping the likes and dislikes of people in mind. I was aware that I had to keep some cuisines besides the Rajasthani ones as well. Thus, we included other cuisines like Chinese and Italian too.

The next challenge was to find cooks who knew how to prepare excellent Chinese and Italian food. We gave ads in the newspaper and got many calls. We invited them all and took a small test to see how they cooked. All of them were quite average, however. Not a single cook came close to preparing noodles even half as good as I did. Only five days were left, and I still found myself struggling with getting a good cook.

Saxena uncle used to call me often to ask about the progress of Sampoorn. That day too, he called me up. I picked up the call and said, 'Hello, uncle.'

'Hi, Mehak beta. Has your interior work finished, or is it still in progress?'

'Yes, uncle. It's finished and the place looks awesome. When are you coming to Kota to see the interiors?'

'Very soon, beta. Only four days are left before the inauguration, you must be so excited.'

I was more tensed than excited, so I replied, 'Uncle, I am still struggling to find a good cook.'

In no time, uncle shouted, 'What, why didn't you tell me this before?'

I was shocked when I heard his words. I replied, 'Do you know somebody?'

He said smilingly, 'You remember my daughter Shivangi? You might have met her at Vaibhav's wedding…'

I replied, still confused, 'Yes.'

'She is a very nice cook. She just completed her hotel management course and is looking for a job. I can talk to her if you want.'

I stammered, 'That's good uncle, but is she willing to work at a new restaurant? She can get a better job at some good established restaurant, I am sure.'

'She will get a chance to prove herself at your restaurant. This is how this industry works, she said, which is why she is looking for new upcoming restaurants. If I had known that you were looking for cooks, I would have told you this long ago.'

'If that is the thing, then send her tomorrow itself,' I smiled.

Uncle laughed and said, 'She is in Kota only, at her sister's place.'

I laughed and replied, 'That's awesome, tell her to come right away.'

A few hours later, Shivangi came to my restaurant with her resume in hand. I smiled at her and said, 'You are a true professional Shivangi, there is no need for a resume here.'

'Can you please cook something for me?' I smiled and asked her.

She nodded and went to the kitchen. A few minutes later, she came out with a bowl of noodles. They were nicely plated and smelled awesome. Even before taking the first bite, I could tell that they would be delicious. I knew I had found my cook. I quickly offered her the job and said, 'I can only offer you 10,000 rupees plus incentives at this point. It's just a start-up restaurant, I hope you understand that.'

'Not an issue, Mehak. When Sampoorn becomes famous and starts getting long queues outside, I'll ask you to increase my payment.' I laughed and said, 'I am keeping my fingers crossed,' and we both burst into laughter.

***

At last, the big day came. We had done all the marketing that we could afford. We gave leaflets in the newspapers, not just for one day, but for three days continuously. We put hoardings on the roads. I had invited all the people I knew in Kota, including my old office's staff, our mess workers, all the workers of Ganga, Yamuna, Sarasvati, Narmada & Jhelum, all the principals of colleges, even Mr. Sharma, and last but not the least, Karthik's whole family.

Karthik's grandfather cut the inaugural red ribbon and we all entered our newly opened Sampoorn for the first time. That day, the food was free for everybody who came to Sampoorn. It was a big party. Everyone who came in, congratulated me. All of us had especially bought new clothes for that big occasion. Saurav was there with Moksha and they looked great together. I was talking to everybody one by one, telling them the specialties of Sampoorn, when suddenly, I saw a guy clicking pictures. I was a little shocked and went to him. 'Excuse me, sir, do I know you?' I asked.

He greeted me and said, 'Are you Mehak?'

Still confused, I replied, 'Yes.'

'Congratulations, Mehak, for this lovely rooftop restaurant. I am Santosh from Rajasthan Patrika.' He showed me his identity card.

I wanted to ask him who invited him, but I didn't, as he was from a leading newspaper. I smiled at him and said, 'Thank you for coming, please have lunch before you leave.'

I got busy attending to the guests again. Everyone told me how they enjoyed the food. On the first day, I didn't keep many dishes to serve, but just a typical Rajasthani Thali with Baati, Daal and Churma, like the one I had eaten at Shekhawati. As expected, Bhola Ji had done a terrific job and all the guests were licking food off of their fingers. After hearing so many compliments from the guests, Saurav came to me and said, 'You clever girl, you brought the awesome traditional taste from a small dhaba to our city where everyone can enjoy it.'

Saurav was right, that had precisely been my aim. I knew Shekhawati was not such a popular restaurant and Bhola Ji was not a very famous cook. Yet, Bhola Ji had extraordinary talent in cooking which just needed a little exposure, and that was what I gave him.

A few minutes later, I saw another guy clicking pictures. Now, I was even more baffled. I went to him and asked, 'Excuse me, sir. May I help you?'

He said he was from Dainik Bhaskar and covering a story on new food trends in Kota. I was confused as to who invited them. The only name I could think of was Saurav. He was busy playing with Sahil, Khushboo and her dog. I tapped on his shoulder and said, 'Sir, will you please tell me who invited these reporters?'

He looked at me and replied, 'First, you tell me, are you happy seeing these reporters here or not?'

'Obviously, it's good for the restaurant's publicity,' I said.

He winked, 'I invited them.'

I jabbed him with my finger and said, 'Thank you.'

The entire day passed like that. We clicked many pictures of the inauguration party. At the end of the day, we came home tired but happy that the inauguration ceremony had gone so well and that everybody liked the food. The next day was the first day of Sampoorn as a public restaurant. I was excited and thrilled about the kind of crowd that we would get.

The next morning, I was still in deep sleep when I felt my phone vibrating under my pillow. I tried to ignore it as much as I could, but it kept on disturbing my sound sleep. At last, I gave up and looked at it. Saurav had been calling me again and again. I picked up the call and said, 'What, Saurav? Did God send you to earth just to disturb my sleep?'

He giggled and replied, 'Yes, Miss. Lazy. Go and check today's newspaper.'

I confusedly thought, the newspaper? I suddenly remembered something and shouted, 'Oh! The newspaper! You mean, Sampoorn is mentioned in today's paper?'

Saurav sniggered and replied, 'Not in one, but two newspapers!'

I ran out like a mad girl and opened the newspapers. I turned the pages as fast as I could and shouted, 'Idiot, you didn't tell me the page.'

Saurav laughed again and replied, 'Do I have to tell you everything? Go search on your own.' He then paused for a few seconds, trying to create some suspense and finally said, 'Page 3.'

I quickly opened page three and at the bottom left corner, I found a nice picture of Sampoorn. I quickly read the article, 'The fast developing city of Kota is witnessing a fast parallel growth in its quality and quantity of restaurants. Yesterday, I witnessed the opening of our first rooftop restaurant, Sampoorn. You can judge that Kota's restaurant industry is evolving by the sort of novel interiors and quality food that they have started serving. Now, the curious part is to see whether the residents of Kota will like it or not.'

I shouted in excitement, 'Thanks, Saurav!'

I showed it to mom and everybody else at Sampoorn. That column in the newspaper had given us the required boost, and on the first day itself, Sampoorn was almost full with customers. It was a splendid day. We took feedback from the customers regarding the food, the ambience, and any other improvements that they thought we could make.

We started the concept of giving feedback forms along with the bill, so that we would know what to improve.

***

One night, after a long tiring day, I had a dream.

I was walking through some corridor, totally clueless about where I was. I was restless and kept on walking. I saw a board which looked a little blurry from a distance. I started running towards that board and saw ICU written on it. I looked around, but I couldn't see anybody. When I opened the door to the room, I was stunned. There was a bed in that room, and Karthik was lying on it. I looked at him, utterly confused. I had no idea how I had gotten there. Karthik stretched his hand towards me and I went closer to him. He wanted to speak, but he was struggling. He stammered, 'I'll come in your life again.' I held his hand and started crying.

Suddenly, I woke up and found my eyes filled with tears. I was sweating heavily. Karthik's words kept echoing in my head, 'I'll come in your life again.' I wondered what it meant. I was too tired to think at that point of time, so I slept again, hoping that his words would come true and I would find him again.

***

Time passed by. In about a year and a half, Sampoorn began to be counted amongst one of the best restaurants in Kota. Bhola Ji proved to be a rock star. Everyone loved his cooking. According to the customers, the food he prepared gave a very ethnic taste of Rajasthan, which was very rare to find anywhere else. Shivangi was the most popular chef amongst the youngsters. Her experimental new dishes were loved by them who loved to eat junk food like pizzas and burgers.

With an increasing demand by the customers, we started a home delivery service. That increased our profits by 20%. Most importantly, it expanded our reach.

I bought a new home for us, with more rooms and ample space. Everyone got their separate rooms. Sahil and Khushboo chose their rooms to be painted in their favourite colours. As promised, I finally gifted mom a big puja room where she could sit and conduct her prayers. We all missed dad and often thought how happy he would be, had he been with us. Khushboo was an excellent student and was preparing for IIT along with her board exams. She understood our family situation and had started concentrating on studies, which helped her score 97% in class 10th.

Mom and I had full confidence that she would undoubtedly crack IIT-JEE. She was also confident that she had put in all the necessary effort in preparing for it. Her board exams finally arrived and as a result of her hard work, she got 95% in boards.

Khushboo had appeared for various examinations such as IIT and AIEEE, and we were eagerly waiting for the results. A month later, all the results got announced one after the other. She had scored a good rank in IIT & AIEEE, which was 5014 and 300 respectively, good enough to get her into an excellent college.

Moreover, Khushboo had also applied for an engineering scholarship programme at MIT, and appeared for SAT & TOEFL. She had always wanted to go abroad and study, so that she could change the way the society thinks about girls making their career and reaching the heights of success.

We kept our fingers crossed for the results.

I was at Sampoorn one day, busy recording the day's collection, when I saw Mehak running towards me. She was shouting and attracting the attention of all the guests who were enjoying their dinner.

She was loud enough for them to stop eating and look at her in shock.

Breathing heavily, she tried to say something.

'Calm down, Mehak, and sit down first,' I said.

'Didi, I scored 2350 in SAT and 1590 in SAT II.'

I was clueless about what that meant and it showed on my face.

She shouted with full energy again, 'With this score, I can get into MIT.'

I couldn't control my happiness and screamed in excitement, making the guests all the more concerned about what was happening.

Soon, she received a letter from MIT, congratulating her for the selection and giving intimations about the fees, etc. We looked at the fees structure. I was shocked to see that the fees were amounting to about 40,000 USD for one year. I became tensed and worried. Mom was tensed too. She thought for two minutes and said, 'We can't afford this much fee. Why don't you take admission in some good college in India itself?'

I looked at Khushboo, she didn't look convinced with mom's words. She retorted, 'Mom, MIT is the world's best college. How can you compare it with Indian colleges?'

I knew she was right, but 20 Lakhs a year was a big amount. Even after excluding the scholarship that she had got, we still had to pay a total amount of 50 lakhs for her full course. That was anyhow beyond our capacity. Even if I included all my savings, I could hardly arrange Rs. 20 Lakh. I looked at Khushboo and saw a few tears in her eyes. I comforted her and said, 'We'll find out a way, beta. You don't worry.'

When she left the room, mom said, 'She is getting such good colleges in India too, why does she want to go to the U.S.?'

I replied, 'Mom the level of studies there is far more advanced and better than in India.'

'Mehak, you have been working so hard since you were just 16 years old. I can't let you spend all the money that you've earned over these years,' Mom replied angrily.

'Mom, the circumstances during that time were different. I didn't have an option, so I did what was necessary,' I replied.

'Whatever it is, but when she can study in India, there's no sense in spending so much money and sending her to the U.S. That's final.'

I held mom's hands and said, 'Mom, when papa died and I watched you struggle for even a meaner sum daily. and saw Sahil and Khushboo craving for every little thing, I promised myself that I would give you all the happiness you deserved. Khushboo really wants to go to MIT and I don't want to suppress her desires.'

Mom started crying and replied, 'I didn't realize when you became so mature.'

I got ready and left for work. I was puzzled and didn't know what to do. In such situations, there was only one man I always counted on, Saurav. I called him up and told him everything. He suggested that we take a loan from the bank and then pay back the instalments every month.

We decided to contact some banks for the loan. The next day, Saurav came home in the morning and we went to a private bank where I used to deposit all my restaurant's earnings. We went to the bank manager and told him about the amount I required. He carefully looked at the fee structure and said, 'No issues, you'll get a loan.'

I smiled. He continued, 'You'll have to deposit your house papers as guarantee though.'

I didn't have any problem in depositing my house papers as guarantee, so I smiled and said, 'Sure, that's not a problem. What about the monthly EMIs?'

He carefully calculated the percentage and replied, 'Rs. 50,000 a month.'

I was shocked and puzzled. I thanked the bank manager and left. Saurav was shocked too and suggested that I drop the idea. We started thinking of a different way to arrange for the money, but whatever I thought of was very costly.

A week passed. Khushboo and I were getting more restless day after day. One day, I was at Sampoorn, instructing Bhola Ji and Shivangi about recruiting more waiters. Suddenly, I got a call from Saurav. He laughed and said, 'Mehak, can you come to my home right now?'

I replied bewildered, 'What happened?'

'Yesterday, I was telling dad about your problem. He just told me that he is willing to lend you the money, but first, he wants to meet you,' he sniggered.

I shouted, 'Are you serious?'

'Yes.'

'I am coming right now.'

I knew that his dad was rich and would have no problem in lending me 50 Lakhs. I called Khushboo up and said, 'Beta, you will go to MIT and this is my promise.'

She shouted with excitement and I could almost see her dancing. I said, 'You'll be so happy. I'll see you in the evening. I love you.'

I reached Saurav's house. His dad was sitting in his office. I went in and greeted him. He smiled and said, 'What is this, Mehak? If you have a money related problem, you should have come to me directly. You are like my own child.'

I thought, 'How generous he is!' I thanked God for having made such people. His dad continued, 'How much money do you want?'

I stammered, '30 Lakhs.'

'But you needed 50, right?' Saurav interrupted and looked at me.

'I have 20 Lakhs, I just need the remaining 30.'

His dad thought for a minute. There was pin drop silence in the room. I was eagerly waiting for his dad's reply. After about five minutes of killer suspense, his dad said, 'Okay, I'll give you the money, but…'

He paused again. Saurav looked at his dad curiously and asked, 'But what, Paa?'

He looked at Saurav and replied, 'Beta, I am a businessmen. Usually, I take 10% interest from everyone that I lend money to. Just because Mehak is a part of the family, I am ready to give her the money without any interest. All I need is your restaurant's papers as security.'

Saurav looked at me in confusion, then he looked at his dad and said, 'Dad, but you said you would help her.'

'Isn't this helping?' he asked Saurav.

I simply stood there puzzled. His dad looked at me and said, 'It's just for the sake of accounts. You don't worry, I am here. Whenever you return the money, you can take the papers back.'

I trusted Saurav very much and I knew he would never advise me to do anything wrong, so I looked at him, hoping to get some reply. There was pin drop silence for a few minutes again. Saurav looked at me and was about to say something, but his dad interrupted and said, 'Mehak, don't worry. This way, you are saving on the interest that anyone else would charge. I am your well-wisher.'

I knew he was a genuine man and above all, he was Saurav's father. How could Saurav's father do anything wrong. I tried to smile and said, 'I know, uncle, you are my well-wisher. I am okay with your conditions.'

Saurav was still thinking something and looked very serious. I looked at him and asked, 'What happened?'

He smiled and said, 'No, nothing.'

His dad looked at me and said, 'So, when do you want the money?'

A week remained to submit the fees, so I replied, 'As soon as possible.'

'Don't worry, bring the papers and take the money in cash,' he replied convincingly.

I thanked him and left. When I reached home, Khushboo came running to me and hugged me. She was crying. I asked curiously, 'Why are you crying?'

Wiping her tears, she replied, 'I love you, Di.'

I patted her on the head and said, 'Go and make us proud.'

The next day, I went to Saurav's house and asked one of the servants, 'Where is Saurav?'

'He is not at home,' she politely replied.

I texted him, 'Hi, where are you? I am at your place.'

I went to his dad's office. He looked at me, smiled and said, 'Come, come, Mehak. I was just about to call you.'

I asked in a surprised manner, 'Why?'

'I got the cash with me today, so thought I would call you and ask you to come. Have you brought the papers?' he asked soberly.

'Yes,' I said and smiled. I felt my phone vibrating and took it out from the pocket. Saurav had replied, 'Coming in half an hour.'

Saurav's dad took out a suitcase from his almirah and placed it on the table. He looked at me and said, 'Please count it before you leave.'

When I opened the bag, I saw many bundles of 1000 rupee notes. That was the first time I was seeing so much cash at once. I looked at the bundles of notes in a perplexed manner and asked, 'Uncle, how will I count through so many bundles?'

He smiled at me and ushered me towards a machine. He had realised that I didn't understand what to do, and said, 'It's a note counting machine.'

I was surprised and wondered why anyone would keep a note counting machine at his office. He took the suitcase there and placed every bundle into the machine one after the other. He kept on telling me the amount as the machine counted bundle after bundle. When he placed the last bundle at last, I calculated the amount, and it was 30 Lakhs.

I looked at him, smiled and said, 'Thanks for the help, uncle.'

I took the suitcase and turned to go out of the room. Suddenly, I heard Saurav's dad's voice. 'Mehak, you forgot something.'

I turned around in a surprised manner. I looked down and saw the hotel papers still in my hand. I said sorry and gave him the papers. Once out of his house, I was about to start my car when I saw Saurav coming. I said, 'Hi.'

He looked tensed and replied, 'Hi, so you took the money?'

I showed him the suitcase and replied, 'Yes. You don't look happy.'

'No, it's nothing like that,' he stammered.

'Come on, Saurav. I know you very well. There's something you are hiding,' I insisted.

He paused for a minute and replied, 'It's just that I feel tense about how you would repay such a big amount.'

I smiled and replied, 'There was a day when I didn't even have 1000 rupees in my pocket. Somehow, with the blessings of God and Paa, I have reached this position. I am leaving this to destiny too. He, who sits high up in the sky, will take care of me.'

He chuckled and replied, 'Can I please give you a salute?'

'Stop teasing me,' I shrugged.

'No, seriously Mehak, jokes apart, I sometime do want to salute your determination and maturity. I always thought that girls are immature and weak, but you have changed my perception. One day, you will be an ideal for all the girls in our country.'

I smiled and left. The very next day, Khushboo sent her confirmation to MIT. We then started waiting for the invitation letter and other documents from MIT, so we could apply for the U.S. visa. I was happy that Khushboo was going to the U.S. to finally attain her dreams.

My Sister Will Fly High

Our house got a lot emptier when Khushboo went to the U.S. We realized after she left that she was that one member of our family who always kept our house so lively. We couldn't eat properly for many days. Sahil missed her badly. His best friend had parted from him. According to Khushboo, MIT was a beautiful place with a lot of good people. Most importantly, she was enjoying her studies, but she missed home at the same time. This was the first time she had left home. She called us twice, or sometimes thrice a week, keeping us updated regarding her studies, friends and her daily routine.

I felt deeply satisfied that I had kept my promise to myself of never letting Khushboo want for anything. Yet, some part of my mind was still tensed about repaying Saurav's dad's money. I cut all the unnecessary expenses to make sure that I could return his money as soon as possible, but the amount was quite significant. Despite the fact that Sampoorn was in profit and was earning 3-4 lakhs a month, I could hardly deposit enough money.

I started working extra hard to make sure that all things went in perfect order and that our customers were always content with us. Most days, Sampoorn was so full that customers had to wait for their turn to get a table. On weekends, this problem would become tenfold. Customers had to wait for more than half an hour sometimes. I knew this was affecting my business, so I decided to expand the restaurant. The question now was how and where. There was only one place I could think of, which was one floor below the rooftop.

Luckily, Saxena uncle was on board with the idea. He said he was very happy with Sampoorn, thus we added one more floor to our growing business.

This level was fully air-conditioned. Now we could give the customers a choice either to take a table on the rooftop or in AC. With an expenditure of Rs. 40,000 as rent and Rs. 1 Lakh on maintenance, I started getting an extra 3 lakhs a month from Sampoorn, which made our monthly turnover touch 7-8 lakhs in total. I was still under a hell of a lot of pressure. I gradually realized that owing money was the most significant pressure that one could have on their head. I was trying hard to be happy and concentrate on my work, but nothing seemed to help. It was like I couldn't rest satisfied till I had returned all the money that I had borrowed.

The Unexpected Turn

Somehow over the next six months, I was able to deposit half the amount that I had taken from Saurav's dad. I decided to return those 15 lakhs to him, so as to reduce at least half of my burden. Saurav was out of station for some work, so I called his father and took an appointment. As per the discussed time, I reached Saurav's house. His father looked at me and said, 'Come Mehak, how are you?'

I smiled and said, 'I am fine, Uncle. How are you?'

'Very well, expanding my business, what else?' he winked. 'So, why did you want to meet? Do you need more money?' he asked.

I replied as quickly as possible, 'No, uncle. It's not that, I came here to return 15 lakhs.'

Suddenly his expression changed. He stared at me and replied, 'How were you able to arrange so much money so quickly?'

I said nervously, 'I did a lot of savings so that I could return your money as soon as possible.'

I forwarded a cheque of Rs. 15 Lakh to him. Saurav's dad looked at me and said, 'I have a deal for you, Mehak.'

I didn't have any idea what he was talking about, so I asked confusedly, 'What deal?'

He smiled and said, 'Come on. Let's sit and then talk.'

I quietly sat on a chair nearby. He then said, 'Take 20 lakh more and give me your restaurant.'

When I heard that, something jabbed me hard. I couldn't control my emotions and looked at him angrily. 'What are you saying, uncle, how you can even think of that?'

He laughed sneakily and replied, 'You are an immature girl, Mehak. How will you handle such a big restaurant? Accept my offer and take the 20 lakhs.'

I was aghast and admonished him, 'Don't you think like that even in your dreams. I am very much competent at handling my restaurant. You don't worry about it. I'll pay your the full money in a week's time, and you better give me my restaurant's papers back then.'

He retorted, 'Mehak, you are my son's friend, which is why I am offering you 20 lakhs more. Otherwise, I would already have thrown you out from your restaurant.'

I exclaimed, 'It's my restaurant and no one steals it from me.'

'You have one week, Mehak. Either take the 20 lakhs and leave that restaurant, or leave the restaurant without taking a single penny. You choose what you want, I'll send the court order in a week,' he laughed.

I walked out of his house furiously, with a few tears in my eyes. I got into my car and burst into tears. I broke down with the dreadful thought of losing my restaurant. I couldn't think of anything, of what to do or how to come out of that pathetic situation that I was in. I started cursing myself for not listening to mom's advice to have Khushboo study in India. I was worried about telling mom all this. She was not well in the first place and a news like this would have completely broken her down. My mind stopped working and started giving me negative thoughts. I thought, 'Did Saurav set me up? Did he know his dad's plan all along? What if Saurav wants to take full ownership of Sampoorn and cheat me like that?'

My mind and heart started debating with each other, leaving me in absolute confusion. My heart was saying that he could never do such awful things; he was my best friend and always wished the best for me. Whereas, my mind kept saying that money is the most powerful thing in the word and that anyone can be misled by such an amount.

I quickly took out my phone and dialled Saurav's number; I told him of the conversation I had had with his dad. He paused for a few minutes and replied, 'This can't be possible, Mehak. He must be joking.'

I shouted angrily at Saurav, 'Are you crazy, Saurav? Tell me, you didn't know your dad's plan, and you didn't set me up for this.'

He was silent for a minute and replied, 'Mehak, you think I planned this with my dad? How can you think like that?'

'Money is everything these days, above all relations and feelings,' I shouted.

'Mehak, I never cared for money, and this is the reason why I always kept myself out of my dad's business. Believe me, I didn't know this would happen,' he replied desolately.

'I don't believe you, Saurav,' I said and hung up.

I was so angry that I didn't even realize what I had said to Saurav. The only thought I had in my mind was the horror regarding the prospect of losing the restaurant in one week. I decided not to tell this to mom and called Saxena uncle instead. I told him everything. He suggested not to worry and gave me the number of one of the top lawyers of Kota, Mr. Bharat. I was so worried that instead of calling him, I directly went to his office. Upon reached his office, I came across a receptionist sitting in the lobby. I requested her to arrange a meeting with Mr. Bharat. She asked me my name, dialled some number and said, 'Sir, Ms. Mehak is here to meet you.' I suddenly remembered that I had forgotten to give Saxena uncle's reference. I quickly said, 'I am a relative of Mr. Saxena.'

She continued talking into the receiver, 'Sir, she says that she is a relative of Mr. Saxena.'

The receptionist then put the phone down and ushered me in. I went in and saw a stout man sitting in his chair. He greeted me and said, 'Yes Mehak, how can I help you?'

I told him all the necessary details that I could tell, but when I mentioned Saurav's dad's name he interrupted me and asked, 'Is he the one who owns Eatos?'

I replied hesitantly, 'Yes.'

He heard all my concerns and said, 'Mehak, don't worry. He is a good friend of mine. I can arrange for a settlement between you and him.'

Again, I got shocked and replied, 'What settlement, Mr. Bharat? Sampoorn is my restaurant, and I will not let anybody take it from me.'

I soon understood that there was no point in staying there, so I thanked him and left.

I couldn't sleep that entire night. I kept wondering what to do and how to save Sampoorn. The next morning, I quickly got ready and left without saying a word to mom.

When I reached Sampoorn, I spotted Saurav standing in the parking lot and waiting for me. He walked towards and we both stood there for a few minutes, without uttering a single word. Saurav then broke the silence and said, 'Believe me,

Mehak, I didn't do anything. I had never thought in my wildest dreams that my dad could ever do such a thing.'

I could sense truth in his eyes and in the deepest corner of my heart as well, I knew that he could never do such things with his best friend. I couldn't control my tears and hugged him while I broke down. Saurav held my hands and said, 'You are in this problem because of me. If I hadn't forced you into taking money from my dad, this would never have happened. I promise you, Mehak, no one will take your Sampoorn from you. Please trust me.'

'I trust you.'

'Give me two days, I'll surely find some way out,' he replied and left.

***

The next two days passed by with great difficulty. When I got a call from Saurav on the third day, he sounded distressed and said, 'I have fulfilled my promise, I am coming to meet you.'

Half an hour later, he finally arrived and broke the suspense. He smiled at me and handed me a file. I looked at the file in confusion and quickly opened it without wasting any more time. I looked at Saurav in a surprised manner and said, 'These are my restaurant papers. Thank God, your father finally understood that he is doing a wrong thing and returned them to me.'

'He didn't give me back these papers himself. I stole them from his locker,' he replied with a stammer.

'What? Are you crazy? Why did you do that? Your father will hold me responsible for this,' I replied.

'You don't worry about that. I'll handle my father. Although, he might throw me out of the house after this, so I should better start looking for a new house to stay in,' he giggled.

'Saurav, how can you crack such a joke in this serious situation? What has happened to you?'

'You don't worry, dear. My father needs these kind of lessons and he is lucky to be receiving one such from his own son,' he giggled again.

He was laughing, but I was tensed. I replied, 'Whenever I have money, I'll give it back to him. I can never cheat anyone.'

Saurav suddenly shouted and said, 'Hello, Ms. Honest. Don't try to do that. He'll inflict forgery cases on you otherwise.'

***

The next day, Saurav came to Sampoorn and told me how his father had reacted when he came to know of Saurav's actions. As expected, he threw Saurav out of the house and declared that he was not his son anymore. Saurav was smiling when he told me all this. I wondered how one could take such a big step for the sake of their friend. Suddenly, my heart planted an idea in my mind and I hastily said, 'Listen, I have an idea. I owe your dad 30 lakhs, right?'

Saurav nodded his head and replied, 'Yes, so what?'

'You are his son, so I can return the money to you. This way, I'll be satisfied that I at least cleared my debt.'

He started at me and replied, 'You are too much, Mehak.'

We were so involved in this discussion that I didn't notice Bhola Ji standing there and listening to our conversation. I noticed him when he interrupted us, looked at Saurav and said 'Why don't you two mutually invest some amount and open a new restaurant in partnership?'

Saurav and I looked at each other and gave each other a high five.

***

Our next project started very soon and I was happy to finally have Saurav with me as my partner. After a lot of thinking and considering all the ifs and buts, we decided to open our new restaurant in Udaipur, which was also the land of tourists, besides just the 'land of lakes'.

We decided to name this restaurant 'Sampoorn' as well, as the brand had acquired value by now. We also decided to shift Bhola Ji to this new location in order to build the best reputation we could.

Since I had opened the Sampoorn in Kota with a reasonable amount of 10 Lakhs, I was pretty sure that we could do wonders with a more significant amount in our pocket. We went to Udaipur to look for an appropriate location. I found Udaipur very beautiful and rich in natural beauty. We noticed a lot of tourists there too, licking the delicious Indian delicacies off their fingers.

We were in search of a fully furnished place, so we could open as soon as possible. We didn't have much luck while we looked on our own, so we went to a real estate agent and soon found our new place for a reasonable sum of Rs. 20,000 only.

This place was near the lake 'Fateh Sagar'. We stood by the lake-side, beholding the beauty of it, when suddenly I realized that we were there to assess the restaurant location. Curious, I asked the real estate guy, 'Where is the location?'

He pointed to a spot across the lake. I strained my eyes to see what he was referring to. It seemed to be a beautiful wooden structure, built up in the shape of a hut. We walked over to the place to look at it up close. It seemed to be a nice place which held great potential to do wonders if we renovated the interiors a little bit.

We signed the contract for that place that very day. We already knew whom to contact for the interiors, the same guy who had done the interior decoration for Sampoorn in Kota.

Saurav took care of the legal permissions that we needed to open the restaurant.

Our target of opening it in a month was achieved and soon, the day came when we were standing in front of our new restaurant, decorated with colours and lights. Mom was there too and was happy and cheerful to see another addition to my business. After the inauguration that evening, Khushboo called me from the U.S. to congratulate us. She also told me that she was coming to India with her friends and their families for her semester break.

Khushboo told us of their plan. While her friends and their families had planned to spend their time visiting Kedarnath, Badrinath and Rohtang, she wanted to come home and spend time with us. Once they'd done with everywhere else, she wanted to show them the beauty of Rajasthan herself.

Here at the new Sampoorn, we started serving the customers with Bhola Ji's ethnic Rajasthani delicacies which got really popular within the short span of a month. Most of our customers were foreigners. My target customers there were always the foreigners, so I was happy with the response, though I had to instruct Bhola Ji to make the food less spicy. I increased his salary and sponsored his other son's education too.

Mom and I were desperately waiting for Khushboo to come back, as it had been one whole year since she had left for the U.S. Sahil was most excited, making plans after plans with her. Some have said it right, when you are waiting for something, time passes crawls like a caterpillar.

Finally, the day that we had been waiting for arrived. Khushboo told us that her flight would land at the IGI Airport, New Delhi, at 8 o'clock in the morning. We were so excited to meet her that we decided to go to the airport to receive her. Mom and I reached the airport at 9 o'clock. Our eyes scanned the crowd hoping to recognise one of those faces as our cute little Khushboo. Mom kept asking when would she come. I tried her phone, but it was still switched off.

Airports are strange places, a crockpot of various emotions brewing at the same time and at the same place. I saw teary mothers bidding farewell to their children, dads fussing over them to take care and study hard, wives and girlfriends hugging their husbands or boyfriends goodbye or vice versa. And though the ones ready to depart were beaming with the excitement of getting somewhere new, the commonality between both groups of people were the tears. For us human species, tears somehow reign over the most expressive medium to express love, care, and affection.

I was still immersed in my thoughts, when mom suddenly shouted, 'Khushboo beta!'

Coming back to my senses, I looked around for Khushboo. The nearest match for her was a girl coming straight towards us. I observed that she had changed quite a bit. She seemed fairer and her hair was a lighter shade of brown. She had on long boots and a fancy scarf around her high neck pullover. I recalled the day when we had come to the same place to see her off when she was leaving for the U.S. She was just a simple Indian girl then, bidding us goodbye in traditional Indian clothing.

As soon as she came up to us, she hugged me tightly. My eyes grew moist as I smiled and said, 'Welcome to India, choti.' Mom had started crying from the moment she saw her coming out of the arrivals gate. Khushboo hugged mom next and said, 'I missed you, Maa,' and joined our league of teary faces.

Khushboo introduced us to five of her friends and their families. Mom felt a little shy talking to them because of their language and the accent, but she greeted everybody pleasantly with a 'Namaste'. She pulled me aside and pointed towards two of Khushboo's friends, saying, 'What are they wearing?'

I smiled and replied, 'This is how they dress.'

I invited all of them to Kota and Udaipur, and requested them to visit my Sampoorn to get a taste of the Rajasthani food there. Soon after, all of them left for their trip further, while we left for our home. Khushboo was happy to see us and kept telling us all the stories and interesting things about her college and the US. I told her, 'You have changed, choti,' to which she smiled and replied, 'I am the same Khushboo, Di. Your choti.'

For the next week, mom made all of Khushboo's the favourite dishes. I began to feel jealous of her as mom entirely forgot about me, spending all her time taking care of Khushboo and feeding her as much as possible.

A week passed and Khushboo's friends and their families came back to Delhi to explore Rajasthan and the other nearby states. Khushboo left for Delhi to meet up with them. I had already spent two months in Udaipur, so I was back in Kota to take care of my canteens and the restaurant.

Khushboo told us that they had planned on going to Jaisalmer, Udaipur, Jaipur and Mount Abu over the next seven days. I told her to go and have dinner at my restaurant in Udaipur.

One day, I got a call from Khushboo while I was at Ganga, checking the accounts. She said, 'Di, can you come to Udaipur tomorrow?'

I was surprised and asked, 'What happened, is everything alright?'

'Yeah, everything is fine. It is just that Mary's dad wants to meet you,' she chuckled.

I was still puzzled as to why he wanted to meet me, so I asked again, 'Come on, tell me what happened.'

'We had dinner at Sampoorn last night and everyone liked it very much. Suddenly, Mary's dad told me that he wanted to meet my sister, so I said okay.'

'Okay, I'll be there tomorrow,' I replied, still thinking what the matter could be.

I was confused, so I asked Saurav to accompany me. We made the overnight journey and reached Udaipur early the next morning. Khushboo and her friends were staying at a hotel close to Sampoorn, so I called her up and invited all of them to lunch. I instructed Bhola Ji to prepare special 'Bail Gatte', a famous Rajasthani dish. At 1 o'clock, Khushboo arrived at Sampoorn with all the guests. I greeted everybody and introduced them to Saurav. Khushboo, while introducing me to the man who had wanted to meet me, said, 'Di, he is Mr. Mathew, Mary's father. He lives in Massachusetts, Boston.'

'Boston.' This word always did something to me. I automatically found myself struggling with my past. I controlled my expressions and replied smilingly, 'Hello, Mr. Mathew. I hope you're liking your stay in India.'

He guffawed and said, 'India is beautiful and so diverse in terms of climates and cultures. But most importantly, I liked Indian food.'

Everyone there nodded their heads in agreement. I happily replied, 'India is beautiful, full of natural beauty, and the food here is altogether different from other countries, with all the different spices. Today, I have for you a special Rajasthani dish to taste called 'Bail Gatte'.' I then instructed the waiter to serve the food.

Soon, the food was served at the tables. Everyone looked at the dish suspiciously. I understood that they didn't have any idea how to eat it, so I demonstrated it to them. I observed everybody's expression while they took their first bite. When I looked over to Saurav, I found him doing the same. Mary was the first one to compliment. While taking in a spoon-full of Gatte, she said, 'Wow, this taste is so different. I have never tasted anything like it before.'

Mr. Mathew interrupted and said, ‘Who cooked such delicious food?’

I smiled and instructed a waiter to bring out Bhola Ji, and a few minutes later he came out. One of Khushboo’s friends asked, ‘What is that on his head?’ She was referring to Bhola Ji’s turban. I told her that Bhola Ji was wearing a traditional Rajasthani dress. Mr. Mathew asked a few more questions from Bhola Ji, and I had to perform the role of a translator for both of them.

After everyone was done with lunch, I instructed a waiter to bring the famous Lassi for dessert. While sipping his Lassi, Mr. Mathew said, ‘Mehak, I am sure you are wondering why I wanted to meet you?’

I was about to ask him just that, so I inquisitively replied, ‘Yes?’

‘Let me first tell you my background. I am an investor in the U.S., and take interest in different lines of businesses.’

I nodded my head and replied, ‘That’s great. So are you looking to invest some money in India?’

‘No,’ he replied quickly. Saurav and I waited for his next words. After a few seconds, he said, ‘I want to invite you to the U.S. to set up an Indian restaurant there. These days, Indian food is in demand everywhere, especially in the U.S.’

Initially, I couldn’t believe what I was hearing. I exchanged confused glances with Saurav and replied to Mr. Matthew, ‘Are you serious?’

‘Yes, I am very serious. The place will be mine, all the set up will be mine, you just get the team and manage everything. As far as profits are concerned, we can divide them 70-30, 70 mine and 30 yours,’ he said.

I still couldn’t believe that he was giving me an offer to set up an Indian restaurant in the U.S. I was still immersed in my thoughts when he continued, ‘Mehak, believe me, you can earn a lot of profits there in the U.S. Khushboo is like my own kid, and I would be glad to get a chance to do business with her sister.’

I looked at Saurav, and he looked at me. I didn’t know what to say. Everything was taking such an unrealistic turn, that my mind was confused. I didn’t know why but one question came to my mind and I asked, ‘What city do you want to open the restaurant at?’ He quickly replied, ‘Boston.’

‘Boston.’ Again, this name echoed in my head. Karthik’s face suddenly flashed across my mind. My heart started to force me to say yes to him. My mind, however, was saying that Saurav is my partner, I can’t decide without asking him. For the first time, I listened to my mind and said to Mr. Mathew, ‘I need a day’s time to think.’

He smiled and replied, ‘Sure, I will wait for your reply.’

After everyone left, only Saurav and I were left behind. I looked at Saurav with eyes asking a lot of questions and expecting so many answers. Thankfully, Saurav understood my concern and said, ‘I think it’s a wonderful opportunity for you to grow your business internationally. You should go.’

Saurav was always so pure of heart, always wanting the best for me. I wished I could get a friend like him for all my seven births. I ran to him and hugged him. ‘If you would have said no, I’d have refused, Saurav.’ He smiled and said, ‘Why would I say no to such a good opportunity? Don’t worry, I’ll take care of the restaurants. You go and make us all proud.’

I called mom and told her every line of the discussion I had had with Mr. Mathew. As expected, she thought it to be an excellent opportunity as well and agreed to it without taking another minute.

Back To The Present Day

'Sumit, are you there? Sumit, hello?' I heard Mehak shouting and trying to pull me back from my thoughts. I looked at my watch, it had been five hours since we came to the cafe called, 'The Station.'

I looked at Mehak as if I had known her for decades. I was speechless. I was looking down when I heard her say, 'So this is my story, Sumit. That is why I am here in Boston.'

I gathered my courage and replied, 'I want to give you a salute, Mehak.' A few tears rolled down from my eyes.

She suddenly exclaimed, 'Hey, Sumit. Why are you crying, yaar?'

Mehak stood up and hugged me. I held her as if I had known her since childhood. I didn't want to leave her, but I had to, so I opened my arms.

I wanted to know more of what happened to Saurav, her mom, Khushboo, Sahil and about everything else which she had not told me. I wiped my tears and asked, 'Where is Saurav, and your mom and Khushboo?'

She smiled curiously and replied, 'Saurav got married to Moksha. He is handling Sampoorn well and gave back those 30 Lakhs to his father. Mom is still in India. I'll bring her here very soon. Khushboo is here in Boston, pursuing her studies. Sahil is pursuing his studies too and before you ask how the food at my restaurant is so good, I would like to tell you that Bhola Ji is here with me.'

I had hundreds of questions in my mind and wanted her to keep on narrating every minute detail of her story.

I didn't want her to stop and said, 'Tell me more about that dream you had about Karthik.'

She smiled and replied, 'You heard my story really closely, I would say. Yes he came to my life again.'

I jumped with happiness and asked, 'When, how, where is he?'

She opened her bag and pulled out a photo from it. She touched the photo to her lips, and I couldn't help but say, 'Come on! Show me, please.' She turned the photo around and my eyes widened on looking at the picture. I asked curiously, 'Who is he?'

She smiled and replied, 'Karthik.'

I was confused and said, 'But this is a small kid.'

'Yes.'

'I had lost a soul which was pure and pious. I couldn't prevent his death, even though I was ready to trade my own life with God to save his life. After Karthik died, I was determined to give life to someone when the time was right. I decided to adopt a kid sometime back and visited an orphanage during my last trip to India. It was quite a coincidence, I would say. I was at Salaam Balak Trust to meet the manager. I entered the gate and was crossing through a lobby when I noticed a caretaker trying to calm a small kid down. She was gently patting this baby while humming a song continuously. The baby still continued to sob. The kid was about a month or two old, I guessed. I couldn't resist going to the room and requested the caretaker to hand the kid to me. When she did, I carefully embraced the kid in my arms, considering my inexperience of handling new born babies. 'Cutie pie, why are you crying?' I asked while kissing her on the forehead. She looks straight into my eyes, enough to hypnotised me and to make me fall in love with her with just one glance. Soon enough, she stopped crying and slept peacefully in my arms. I was getting late to meet the manager, so I went to her office, still embracing the baby in my arms.

'Come, Mehak. Oh, where did you find this naughty little angel?' Ms. Malti asked me curiously.

I quickly narrate the entire story to Malti and requested if I could adopt her.

She said, 'He is a boy. Someone left him here a few days ago and we haven't been able to trace out his parents. We found him on 14th February. Our doctors noticed his umbilical cord and told us that his date of birth most probably is 13th February,' and smiled.'

I couldn't believe what she had just said so I asked her again, 'What did you say his date of birth might be?'

'13th February.'

I was stunned 'What? That is the date on which Karthik died.'

'Yes.'

'So? You adopted him?'

'Yes,' she smiled.

'Oh my God, where is he?'

'He is in India with his grandmother.'

Mehak then smiled at me and left. I kept sitting there for an hour, recalling her story and thanking Mehak for this new inspiration she had given me. Suddenly, some words came to my mind, 'Never underestimate girls, particularly The Girl I Know.'